# SWORD OF EGYPT

## BY BERT WILLIAMS
### ILLUSTRATED BY LASZLO GAL

Scholastic Canada Ltd.

*To my mother, Evelyn,*
*and my father, Wesley,*
*who made me all possible*

ISBN 0-590-71058-3

9 8 7 6                    Printed in Canada                    8 9 / 9
                    Manufactured by Webcom Limited

# CONTENTS

# THE GREAT FLEET

Aahmes, son of Horem-heb, sat on a canal bank dangling his feet in the muddy water. To his right he could see the Nile stretch as far as Thebes, the capital of Upper Egypt; to his left it extended even farther — past the city of Luxor, where he lived, all the way to the southern horizon. Behind him the flat plain was broken into tiny square fields that were still under water from the floods. The villages had been moved back from the river during the Season of Inundation while everyone waited for the annual overflow to provide fresh mud for planting. Without the Nile, all would be worthless desert in this land that received so little rain.

Although it was now the Season of Sowing, no one was at work in the fields yet, because the river had not receded enough. It would probably be another month or more, until the very end of Tobi or even the beginning of Mekhir, before the seeds could be planted and the sheep and goats brought into the fields to trample them into the rich earth. Then the peasants would move their villages back nearer to the river.

For four months the plants would grow, and then would come the Season of Harvest, during the month of Pakhons. Some of the crops would be eaten fresh, the remainder dried in the hot sun and stored for the next Season of Inundation, when the whole process would be repeated, as it had been since Geb, the God of Earth, had been born from a flower on the Great Ocean.

It was just as well that no work had started in the fields yet, for the Feast of Opet was about to begin, and this year it was to run for twenty-seven days instead of the usual eleven. The Great One, Ramses III, Pharaoh of Upper and Lower Egypt, son of the Gods Amon-Re and Horus, had decreed it, following the triumph of his latest campaign.

Aahmes was impatient for the festival to begin. He had hurried home shortly after midday, as soon as school was over. Then, stopping only long enough for some *ta,* his favourite kind of bread, and a drink from the huge water jar by the front door, he had run along the canals to this spot. Now he was waiting for the arrival of the Great Fleet.

It was expected sometime that day and he wanted to be the first from Luxor to see it. Several fishing skiffs had already passed, but nothing that could be mistaken for part of the Pharaoh's fleet. When that came into view, it would dot the river with hundreds of ships.

What a glorious sight it would be! The northern breezes would puff out the sails, and the homebound crews would pull on the oars with all their might. Aahmes wished his own feeble strength might be added to theirs, for one of the ships in that magnificent fleet would carry the Great One himself. And standing at his side would be Horem-heb, Aahmes' father, Warrior of the King and Commander of the Shock Troops, who had twice been awarded the Collar of Valour in battle.

Aahmes burned with excitement at the thought of seeing his family. This campaign had lasted only three months, but it had been the loneliest three months he had ever experienced, because for the first time his brother Khepri had gone with Horem-heb as charioteer. Khepri was almost twenty, nine years older than his younger brother, and the time had come for him to march off and fight the Pharaoh's enemies. Aahmes longed for the day when he too would be grown up enough to be a soldier. Then the enemy would truly have a great deal to contend with! He dreamed of a life of adventure and excitement away from home and the temple school, where he was surrounded by strict priests and boys who thought of nothing but playing silly games all day.

During the whole three months there had been no one to talk to at home except the servants, and he couldn't talk to them as he would to his family. A sad expression crossed Aahmes' sun-bronzed face. If only his mother

Nephthys were still alive! Life had seemed so wonderful when she had been there; she had smiled so sweetly and scolded so gently. But two seasons before she had died and gone to the Celestial Fields. That was the place where you were surrounded by your loved ones, so the priests said. But Aahmes couldn't understand that, because he was certain that all his mother's loved ones were still on earth. Religion was mystifying, he concluded, and that was why it took so many priests to explain it.

Again Aahmes wished he were grown up and could take his place beside Horem-heb and Khepri. Like his brother, he would join the chariot corps. If he could work his way up to commanding twenty-five chariots, he would be given the title of Royal Scribe — an honour reserved for the king's own scribes and his chariot commanders. Besides, as a soldier he would not have to sit cross-legged on the ground all day copying out the hieroglyphic symbols that he was learning so laboriously at the House of Life where he went to school.

Every day he and his classmates were given lessons to copy. And Horus help those who made a mistake! Old Senmut, their teacher, did not approve of silliness in children, errors in scribes or laziness in anyone. For each mistake, his students were given further copying to do, and sometimes several blows from the wooden staff he carried.

The lessons were full of statements pointing out the

advantages of a scribe's life: *Be a scribe so that you may be much admired and your limbs may become soft . . . Remember, a scribe pays no taxes, but directs the work of everyone . . . A scribe is not always at the beck and call of many masters, but is chief among all the professions.*

Certainly there was much truth in these sayings. The scribes were the readers, writers and recorders of everything that happened in Egypt. Nothing could be done without their help, because they counted everything, taxed everything, checked everything. It was also true that they paid no taxes; this might explain why they enjoyed taxing others down to the last measure of grain. They even purchased supplies for the royal capital and the army itself, and they claimed that without their work it would be impossible for the state to exist.

What bothered Aahmes was what they said about soldiers like his father. Many of the lessons about army life were simply not true. They were nothing but the silly opinions of jealous scribes — men who could never be soldiers themselves and who refused to acknowledge that the world outside Egypt was filled with enemies. What good would a scribe be if Egypt were invaded?

What was the lesson they had copied that morning? *A soldier must march over the mountains to Syria. He must carry his bread and water on his shoulder like a donkey. By the time he reaches the enemy, he has no strength left in his limbs with which to fight. He may be killed or badly wounded. Do not think then that the life of a soldier is as good as that of a scribe.*

That was wrong, Aahmes told himself. The life for the son of a soldier was to follow his father, to be like him. Anyway, that was the life for him. Then he could defend the Great One and Egypt. If he should fail, surely it was better to die bravely in battle than to hide like a scribe in fear.

But where were those ships? He had been sitting on the bank for hours, and the sun was beginning to sink in the west. What could have delayed them? As soon as they appeared, he would race home and tell the servants to prepare the celebration for the safe return of their master. And what a celebration it would be! Their friends and neighbours would come to pay them honour and everyone would be invited to remain for the feast. Wine and beer made from fermented bread would be served, along with many kinds of meat. Everyone would be happy, and no one would notice if Aahmes remained in the banquet hall to watch. He loved to see the dignified officials unbend after they drank some of the honey-sweet wine. Their wives would enjoy themselves too; some would drink so much that their wigs would begin to slip down over their eyes. Aahmes giggled to himself at the prospect.

He thought of the dancers — especially the Syrian slave girl Anath-herte, whom his father had brought home after the last campaign. She was truly beautiful, and moved with a cat-like grace that he particularly admired. And what an expression her face betrayed whenever she looked at Khepri! Aahmes thought that she cared for his brother more than a slave was supposed to care for a master, but he did not know much of such things.

After the dancers, it would be time for the part of the celebration that Aahmes enjoyed most. His father would send for the blind singer, Uni. Uni would be led into the centre of the room, and a place would be made for him to sit. At first he would remain perfectly still, staring straight ahead with his sightless eyes; then, slowly, he would begin to weave back and forth, singing in a low tone. He knew all the old songs of Egypt that told of brave and wise men who had passed on to the Celestial Fields.

Aahmes had heard him perform so often that he had even learned many of the words. During Uni's sadder songs, tears would come to the eyes of some of the guests. At last Horem-heb would ask him to sing the words that reminded him of his wife:

*Be glad thou mayest cause thine ear to forget*
*that men will one day beautify thee.*
*Follow thy desire, so long as thou livest.*
*Put myrrh on thy head, clothe thee in fine linen,*
*and anoint thee with the genuine marvels*
*of the things of God.*
*Increase yet more the delights that thou hast,*

*and let not thine heart grow faint.*
*Follow thy desire, and do good to thyself.*
*Do what thou requirest upon earth*
*and vex not thine heart*
*until the day of lamentation comes to thee.*
*Yet he with the Quiet Heart hears not their lamentations,*
*and cries deliver no man from the Underworld.*

And at this reminder of the death of the God Osiris, Horem-heb would remain perfectly still, weeping silently. One by one, his guests would quietly leave. Uni would be taken back to his place in the servants' quarters, and the whole household would tiptoe off to bed.

What was that? Aahmes' eye had caught a glint of motion on the river. Could it be the Great Fleet at last?

There! Was that a sail? Yes! And another — and another! The Great Fleet had finally arrived!

Aahmes did not wait any longer. But as he jumped to his feet to start home, he noticed the figure of a young girl bounding along the canal towards him. When she slowed down and leaped gracefully over a runnel of water, he recognized her as Anath-herte.

"Aahmes, master," she called, then paused to catch her breath. "Aahmes, master, you must come at once. Something terrible has happened!"

# A TRAITOR?

Aahmes, recognizing the urgency in Anath-herte's voice, turned at once to run home, leaving her behind. Slaves were always excitable and unreliable sources of information, he reminded himself. It was no use questioning her. He would just hurry back and find out for himself what had happened.

She was a good servant, though, he was forced to admit, and certainly not as flighty and silly as many of the others. She had told him much about her native land, and had even taught him to speak a few words of Syrian. Pharaoh's armies frequently fought in Syria, and a soldier could never know too much about his enemies.

But what could possibly have upset her so? he wondered. He didn't dare put his fear into words. His father? Anyone as brave as his father would be in the forefront of every battle. Besides, he was Commander of the Shock Troops — was it not his duty to lead his men in any attack, or during the besieging of a city? Or Khepri — perhaps something had happened to him. He was just as eager as their father, but not as experienced. He would naturally want to show off his courage during his first campaign, and not shame his father; maybe he had been more daring than was wise. Even worse, Aahmes thought, something could have happened to both his father and his brother.

Aahmes knew the canals well, knew where they could most easily be crossed and where it was possible to go through them without sinking into the mud. He leaped over some, waded through others, and detoured around those he couldn't cross. When he reached open ground, he began to run like the wind.

Although it was already getting dark, he could clearly distinguish his home from some distance away. Unlike the average Egyptian house, it was a grand two-storey structure, surrounded by beautiful gardens and a high white wall. Horem-heb was a very important man and deserved such a dwelling. There was no disturbance near the house that Aahmes could see. Surely if bad news awaited him, all the servants would be milling about the entrance moaning and weeping. But there was no one.

As he drew nearer, he noticed a lone chariot outside the main gate. That could mean a messenger, he thought, or it could indicate that Khepri had come home — alone. That would be a sign that the bad news concerned his father.

At the gate he paused to catch his breath and to try to identify the chariot. Yes, it looked like Khepri's, although he couldn't be sure. The horses' flanks were still heaving from their gallop, so they must have arrived recently. Why hadn't the team been taken to the stables behind the house? Aahmes continued into the courtyard and soon reached the house. There he pulled the leather thong to open the door, and entered the long, columned reception hall. Since it was deserted, he hurried on through the house, past the bedrooms and into the garden at the rear.

The garden had always been his favourite spot, set as it was around a large pool, with palm and sycamore trees providing year-round shade from the hot sun. In the far corner stood the kitchen and the storehouse, and on the other side the stables and servants' quarters were carefully concealed behind rows of trees.

Pacing in front of the pool was Khepri. How changed he is in only three months, Aahmes thought to himself. He seemed so much older and more serious. He was still dressed in his uniform, which was torn and spattered with mud, although the custom was to bathe and change immediately upon returning home. The news must indeed be very bad.

Khepri looked up as his younger brother approached. "Ah, little one," he greeted him, forcing a smile. "I left the fleet downriver so I could hurry home and see you as soon as possible."

Aahmes, seeing the distracted look in his brother's eyes, demanded, "Khepri, what is it? Where is our father, Horem-heb?" He dreaded the answer.

Khepri looked down at Aahmes and placed a hand gently on his shoulder. "Little brother," he began, and then paused. So it really is about my father, the boy thought.

"Aahmes, I have bad news."

"Khepri, please tell me . . . "

"Our father . . . Horem-heb . . . he's . . . " He paused again, as if the words were too heavy to pronounce.

"Please," Aahmes pleaded, hoping with all his heart that his father had not been killed, but perhaps only wounded.

"Horem-heb is dead," Khepri blurted out suddenly.

All the colour seemed to drain from Aahmes' face. He turned from his brother and sank onto the long bench beside the pool. In the glassy-smooth surface of the water his eye caught the reflection of the tall columns that supported the roof of the house. They looked like upside-down lotus flowers. Then a fish disturbed the water and the image began to shimmer and dissolve. His whole world seemed to be rippling away into nothingness.

His father had gone to the Celestial Fields. To join Nephthys? The sadness that had overwhelmed him seemed slightly more bearable at that thought. At least

his parents would be reunited. Had Horem-heb deliberately gone to his death because he could no longer bear being separated from his wife? In the Celestial Fields they would float together down the Nile and await the coming of their sons. What brave deed had his father performed this time? he wondered, pride replacing pain for the moment. Probably something that had saved the Pharaoh's life, or maybe the whole land of Egypt. Yes, it was certain to be such a death that his father had died. He had lived as a hero, and he would certainly have departed in the same way.

"How did it happen?" he asked.

"I will tell you the whole story later," answered his brother. "But first, what about you? How have you been?"

That was just like Khepri. He was the one who was always trying to make up for the loss of their mother by asking Aahmes the sort of questions that she used to ask.

"I have been well," he replied. "But Khepri, please tell me about our father. Tell me the whole story of how he died."

"Aahmes . . . " The tall, bronzed soldier sat down on the bench beside his brother and threw his arm around him. "You know," he remarked, changing the subject again, "you really are growing very rapidly. Each time I do this, my arm rests higher."

"Khepri!"

"Yes, yes, I will tell you. But let's go into the reception room. There is much you must know, and I may not have a great deal of time left." Aahmes did not understand what his brother was saying, but he rose obediently and followed him into the house.

They entered the room, windowless to keep out the heat of the sun, and Aahmes sat on the raised hearth near the shrine dedicated to the black-skinned God, Min. Khepri rested beside him on a pile of cushions, propping himself up on one arm. For a moment he shut his eyes, then blinked them open again. "Aahmes, do you know," he began, "what becomes of the dead who are not properly prepared for burial?"

"Certainly," answered Aahmes impatiently, failing to see the point of such a question. "There is no afterlife for one who isn't properly prepared and buried with all the necessary prayers."

"Exactly. And whose duty is it to see that all this is done?"

"The sons of the dead."

"Well, the eldest son anyway."

"Yes, I know all this." Aahmes could not make sense of this strange conversation and was beginning to think that Khepri's mind must be wandering. Undoubtedly the shock of losing their father had been hard on him. He might even have seen it happen. Still, if it had taken place in Syria, he should have recovered a little by now. "Brother, how did our father die?" he asked abruptly.

Khepri looked guiltily away. He said nothing for so long that Aahmes almost thought he had fallen asleep. Finally he spoke. "You are the son of a soldier, and as such, you know most of the rules of the army."

"Of course. I'm going to be a soldier some day myself, just like you. And as my father was," he added.

Khepri ignored these words and went on. "Do you know what happens when someone is caught carrying weapons in the immediate vicinity of the Pharaoh's sleeping quarters."

"Yes. He's killed on the spot." Aahmes still did not understand the conversation, but a feeling of horror was beginning to creep over him. "Brother, you don't mean . . . "

"Yes, Aahmes. Horem-heb, our father, was found carrying a sword in the presence of the sleeping Pharaoh. He was cut down by Ramses' guards."

"But," the boy protested, "our father would not have done the Great One any harm!"

"Of course not!" Khepri exploded, rising and beginning to pace about the room. "But the guards have their orders and they struck him down. By the time the Pharaoh wakened, it was too late."

"But what was he doing there?"

"I — I don't know," the other admitted. "Anyway, he's been declared a traitor, and it's been decreed that he is to have no burial."

"Oh, no! That means his body will be fed to the

crocodiles," the boy wailed.

"Yes, and there'll be no journey to the Field of Rushes and the Field of Offerings. Our parents will not be reunited in the next world," Khepri added.

"What can we do?" asked Aahmes. "Surely the Pharaoh knows our father must have had a good reason for what he did."

"But Horem-heb is dead. How can the Great One admit that his guards made a mistake? Besides, the law is precise. No one but the royal guards may bear weapons where the Pharaoh sleeps."

"Then what are we to do?"

"You are to do nothing," Khepri told him. "But I — I have made up my mind to see that our father receives a proper burial."

"You mean, defy the orders of the Great One?" The boy sprang to his feet to face his brother.

"I have no choice, little one."

"But you can't. The Pharaoh sees everywhere. He travels across the heavens every day in the shape of Horus. What will happen if he finds you and sends his soldiers to capture you?"

"I suppose I'll be thrown to the crocodiles too."

"Oh, Khepri, it's wrong to defy the Great One."

"It's also wrong to leave one's father unburied," snapped his brother.

"But you owe a duty to obey — "

"And a duty to see that my father's remains are

properly cared for. Now that's enough. I'll do it tomorrow — and I don't think I'll be caught. I'm going to return to Thebes in the morning for Horem-heb's body, then ride out into the desert and bury him as best I can. The prayers will have to wait until later."

"Has he not already been fed to the crocodiles?"

"I arranged for a substitute. Our father's body is safe for now. Don't worry, brother, I'll be as careful as possible. After all," he added, forcing a weak smile, "I'm responsible for you and the estate now." He rumpled the boy's hair.

Looking very worried, Aahmes began to protest, but he was interrupted by a slight noise at the door. As he rose to his feet to investigate, Hemon, the head steward, came into the room. For many years, since before Khepri was born, Hemon had managed the entire household for Horem-heb. He was extremely efficient, making all the necessary day-to-day arrangements, especially since the death of Nephthys. Although Aahmes had never really liked him, he had come to realize that, since he couldn't expect to like everyone, what mattered was that Hemon was a good worker. This understanding, however, had not changed his distrust of the steward. Even now he felt that the man had been standing outside the reception hall listening to the whole conversation between himself and his brother. Perhaps he should inform Khepri of his suspicions.

"Young masters," Hemon began, "will you be eating

at home this evening?" Even his voice conveyed a quality of sneakiness.

A worried frown passed over Khepri's face, as though he too suspected the steward of eavesdropping. "No, Hemon. I am too tired to eat anything. But please see to all my brother's wants."

"Certainly, young master," the other murmured.

"And Hemon," Khepri continued, "if anything should happen to me, you are to serve and obey Aahmes. Is that clear?"

The steward glanced from one to the other with a look of wary calculation. Then he answered, "I will serve the young master as I would serve you, and as I served your father." Without another word, he turned and glided from the room.

"I think he overheard us, Khepri."

"Yes, Aahmes, he may well have done so. I can't say I've ever really liked him, but he has been a good servant. He's not likely to betray our trust." Khepri yawned and rubbed his eyes. "I must get some rest now. I'm tired and I've a busy day ahead of me tomorrow."

Aahmes wished his brother a good night and went to his room. He lay down on the low bed, but for some time tossed and turned in the gathering darkness, trying to weigh the loyalty owed to the Pharaoh against that owed to one's family. Finally he drifted into a fitful, troubled sleep, without discovering an answer to his question.

# AT THE TEMPLE

The next morning, Aahmes awoke later than usual. The servants were already up and busy at their regular tasks, some of them looking worried and upset. Obviously they had heard about Horem-heb's death and wondered how it would affect their lives. Servants and slaves were all the same: their only real concern was for their own welfare.

Khepri had apparently left the house some time earlier. Aahmes hurried back to his own room, took his belted loincloth and papyrus sandals from the box at the foot of the bed, and dressed rapidly. He did not stop for anything to eat, since he was already late leaving for school. He closed the gate carefully behind him, ran to the corner and turned into the street that led to the Temple of Life, where classes were held for the sons of the men who served the Pharaoh.

Aahmes stayed well over to one side to avoid the ditch that ran down the centre of the street. Seeing several of his classmates ahead of him, he ran to catch up. They stopped when he first called to them, but as soon as they saw who it was, they began to walk away. When Aahmes came up beside them, out of breath from running, they ignored him.

"Good morning, Ranofer," he began.

Ranofer stared down at the ground and continued to waddle along as rapidly as his short legs would carry his fat body.

Aahmes could not understand what was wrong. "Ranofer, it's me, Aahmes, son of — " The words stuck in his throat. Was it possible that they too had heard about his father? Was that why they wouldn't speak? Something was certainly the matter. He looked searchingly into the faces of the other two, Baba and Hori. Neither said a word.

Well, that was fine with him. If they wanted to act in this foolish manner, he didn't care. They weren't particularly good friends of his anyway. He had other, much closer companions. He left them, running on ahead. Wait until he saw Kames. Kames wouldn't pay any attention to silly false reports about his family.

The courtyard of the temple was filled with people. Most of them were priests, including the High Priest himself on his way to make offerings to the Gods. He was easy to recognize because of the ceremonial leopard skin and pleated skirt he wore. There were also a number of students. Just starting to climb the steps to the classroom was Aahmes' best and oldest friend.

"Kames," he called out, "wait for me."

The boy paused, looked around as though ashamed of something, and then waited until the other caught up.

"Kames, how are you?"

"I — I'm well," was the reply. "Quite well."

"That's good." Strangely, Kames did not also enquire after his health as was customary. "And your parents?" Aahmes persisted.

"They too are well," Kames answered stiffly. "I think we'd better hurry or we'll be late."

Old Senmut, their teacher, considered tardiness akin to laziness and punished both in the same manner — with blows from his staff. Aahmes was just as concerned about being prompt as his friend was, but surely they had time to talk a little before classes began. What was wrong? Kames kept darting glances around as though afraid of something. Is he ashamed of being seen with me? Aahmes wondered.

"What's the matter, Kames? Tell me the truth."

"How can you talk about truth when you come from a family that doesn't know the meaning of the word?" his friend blurted out, almost shouting.

"What are you talking about?"

"Your father — he betrayed the Great One."

"Kames! . . . Do you really believe that?"

"Of course I do — it's true, isn't it?" countered the other. "He tried to kill the Pharaoh as he slept."

"That's a lie!" cried Aahmes.

"Sure!"

"Do you take the word of others over that of your best friend?"

"Best friend? The son of a traitor?"

"Don't say that!" Aahmes was losing his temper. Who did Kames think he was to say such things? His father was nothing but a scribe in the tax department, and not a particularly high one at that. There were no soldiers at all in his family.

"It's true," Kames shouted again. "Your father was a traitor and he got what he deserved."

"No! It's a lie — and unworthy of you. Take it back."

"I won't. And you can't make me. Everybody knows it. Your father was a trait — " Before he could finish, Aahmes lashed out with his fist, catching his friend across the mouth. Kames fell backwards on the steps, blood trickling from the corner of his lip. A look of surprise and disbelief spread over his face. "You — you hit me," he managed.

"And I will again if you don't take back what you said."

"I'll say what I want. It's the truth," Kames repeated. Slowly he rose to his feet, forcing Aahmes to back away. Then, flailing his arms wildly, he rushed in to attack. When he was close enough, Aahmes hit him again, knocking him down. His friend-turned-enemy lay on the steps, bleeding from both corners of his mouth now, amazement written all over his features.

"You — you — you'll be sorry for this! You'll have to leave school," he screamed. "Who wants to go to school with the son of a . . . " But he paused there, not anxious to be struck again.

By this time a crowd of boys had gathered, urging them to continue the fight. But their wish for more action was interrupted by a deliberate and heavy step that everyone recognized.

"It's Old Senmut!" someone shouted. The crowd melted away, but Kames still lay on the steps. Not sure what to do, Aahmes remained where he was.

Old Senmut strode towards them, his staff in one raised arm. He paused when he recognized them. "Why, it's you, Aahmes. And *you,* Kames. What's this all about?"

"I — I fell," Kames offered.

"You fell? Or were you pushed?"

"No, master. I did fall."

"Yes — with a little help perhaps. Go on into the building."

"Yes, sir." The boy rose shakily to his feet and hurried inside. Aahmes moved to follow, but found his path blocked by the teacher's staff.

"Wait, Aahmes. Did you start the fight?"

"I — I struck the first blow," he admitted. He looked up into the heavily lined face. Was there a trace of kindness there that he had never noticed before?

Senmut gazed at him for some moments without speaking and then said, "You'd better get inside too. Hurry now." Without another word, Aahmes entered the building and took his place, cross-legged, among the others.

His classmates were already busy practising the hieroglyphs or 'priest's writing' that would qualify them for positions as scribes. Each was provided with a fibre brush, ink and a piece of broken pottery to write on. Aahmes carefully removed several hairs from the end of his brush so that his writing would be as fine as possible. Before him was another message intended to induce students to enter the royal service. It read: *Be a scribe so that your limbs may become soft, that you may go forth, admired, in white attire, and that courtiers may salute you.*

But Aahmes' mind was far from such thoughts. He was preoccupied with the problems of his family and could not concentrate on his work. Instead, he began to doodle on his piece of pottery, just to appear busy. He was thinking about his mother. Without realizing it, he made the hieroglyph that stood for the word *beautiful:*

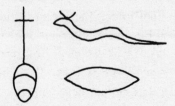

Then beside it he drew the picture of a seated woman, thus changing the meaning to *young girl*.

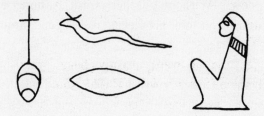

He stopped to admire his brushwork. Anyone could be a scribe if he really wanted to, he decided. But *he* didn't want to. He was going to be a soldier, just like his father.

Tears welled up in Aahmes' eyes. Just then he became aware of Old Senmut standing over him with his hands on his hips. Now he was in for it. He had been daydreaming and would surely be struck with the staff. He waited for the blows, but for some reason they did not fall.

The old priest continued to gaze at him for some time, and then ordered the rest of the class outside to play. As soon as they had left, he turned back to Aahmes. "Do you not think it unwise to continue coming to school under the circumstances?" he asked. "Your father has been charged with a very serious crime."

# OLD SENMUT'S ADVICE

So Old Senmut knew. By this time everyone in Upper Egypt must have heard the story. Aahmes did not know what to say. Maybe he should not have come to school today. Perhaps tomorrow . . .

But he had to defend Horem-heb. "My father meant no harm to the Great One," he told his teacher. "He had served him loyally for years. He — he was there to protect the Pharaoh," he finished lamely.

The priest smiled. "It is good to have faith, little one. I knew your father. I too find it difficult to believe the charges that have been laid against him."

Aahmes looked up in wonder. Someone else believed in Horem-heb, someone outside the family. His hope was renewed. "Oh, master, is there any way we can reach the Pharaoh and convince him?"

The old man looked down at his sandals. "Now wait, boy. I said I didn't believe the charges against him. That does not mean I can prove his innocence. Can you?" At the boy's silence, he went on. "I am nothing but an ordinary priest who has been assigned the task of training scribes. And even if I had proof that would clear your father's name, I couldn't just walk over to the palace and ask to see the Pharaoh."

The boy blinked back tears.

"Besides," the priest continued hurriedly, "have you not heard? There has been more trouble and fighting along the Libyan frontier. Ramses left early this morning to try to stop it before it spreads."

Aahmes' hopes hit rock bottom. Not only was he without proof, but even if he had some, there was no one to present it to. "I understand," he said miserably.

"I'm sorry. I would like to help you, but there's nothing I can offer except advice."

Yes, advice! Priests and scribes were good at offering that. What would Old Senmut have to say? Would he urge Aahmes to study to be a scribe? And when the boy refused, what would he say then? *Thou art like a broken steering oar in a ship that is obedient on neither side.* Then would he explain how to become successful? *Fortunate is the scribe who is skilled in his calling . . . Persevere every day, and thus shalt thou obtain mastery over it . . . Spend no day in idleness, or thou shalt be beaten. The ears of a boy are on his back, and he listens when he is beaten . . .* Yes, he had memorized all the wise sayings — he had had to copy them so often.

He wanted to tell his teacher that such advice had little to do with real life; its only value was to provide something for the boys to copy as they practised the magic writing. But to speak his mind would be rude and disrespectful. Instead, he said meekly, "I am ready to hear, master."

"I was just thinking of an old quotation: *The fame of a man valiant in his deeds shall not perish in this land forever.*"

Yes, that made sense, thought Aahmes. Horem-heb would certainly be remembered for his courage and service. But then the boy remembered some other old sayings about the afterlife. There was one about the noble and the glorified resting in their pyramids, as did the Gods: *But what has happened to the houses they built? Their walls have been destroyed, and their houses are no more.*

And there was a song that Uni sang:
*None returneth from the land of the dead*
*that he may tell us how they live there,*
*that he may tell us what they are in need of,*
*that their hearts may be set at rest,*
*until we go to the place*
*from where there is no return . . .*

There again was the problem. "Master, they have not allowed our father to be properly buried in his own tomb and with the necessary prayers."

The priest expressed surprise. "Of course," he said

then. "Those condemned as traitors are denied the usual rites."

"Do you not think that Horem-heb should be sent to the land beyond Egypt so that Osiris may judge the pureness of his heart? The God of the West will know that he is innocent and permit him to travel to the Celestial Fields to join our mother."

"Ah, I had forgotten that Nephthys had left the Two Lands. This new tragedy must be all the more difficult for you to bear. Have you not a brother though?"

"I have. Khepri is a charioteer."

"I see. Another soldier. Is he in Luxor?"

"Yes, master. He returned last night with the army from Asia."

"Good. Then he'll do something about the problem. I'm afraid, though, that young soldiers are seldom the best thinkers . . . "

"My brother is a good soldier and a wise man," Aahmes offered in his defence.

"Yes, of course he is. I didn't mean to imply that he wasn't. But he's young, and army life does not encourage much contemplation."

"There's more to life than being afraid and thinking all the time and worrying about having soft hands and how little work you can do," the boy snapped.

"What? Ah, I see we have not impressed you with our advice and instructions concerning a career in the royal service. I suppose you plan to be a soldier like your father and brother?"

"Yes, I do. There is more than one way to serve the Pharaoh."

"True. Soldiers are needed too. But all this doesn't help us to decide what should be done with you right now."

"What do you mean, master?"

"I'm talking about the fight you had with Kames, your best friend. When I arrived to break it up, most of the other boys were urging him to get up and beat you — "

"I'm stronger than Kames."

"Perhaps so. But are you strong enough to fight all the students in the school? Were any of them friendly to you? Did any take your side?"

Aahmes hung his head and admitted that they had all been against him.

"And what," the priest continued, "did they say about your father?"

"They called him — a — traitor."

"And they will do so again tomorrow. What will your answer be then?"

"I will fight again — all of them, if I have to. Every day, if need be."

"There you are. So you see my problem. How can I be expected to teach if such disturbances continue?"

The boy hung his head. Of course Old Senmut was right. He knew the boys would keep on taunting him.

And he would have no choice but to fight. "But what can I do?" he asked uncertainly.

"I have only one suggestion: leave school for a while. Perhaps in a few months — "

"A few months!"

"I'm sorry, Aahmes. It's for your own safety. Besides, the High Priest may have something to say — "

"But why should he bother about a fight in the schoolyard?" interrupted Aahmes.

"It would not be about the fight. Do you know who pays to run such schools as these?"

"Of course — the Pharaoh."

"And do you know what their purpose is?"

"They exist to train loyal citizens . . . " The boy halted in mid-sentence as a horrible realization swept over him.

"Exactly," the priest continued, as kindly as possible. "Loyal citizens. That does not include the sons of men who have been executed as traitors."

"But my father wasn't — "

"My, you certainly do have a hot temper. I can see our moral training has fallen on deaf ears. I didn't say that he *was* a traitor, but that he was executed as one. I'm afraid there will be no place for you here, at least until the Pharaoh has had a change of heart. Besides, your classmates would torment you and you wouldn't be happy. The only way to avoid that is to stop coming — perhaps forever. If you wish to be a soldier, and you seem to have the temper for it, you will not need to be very learned anyway." The teacher smiled as he expressed this low opinion of soldiers.

"So go home for now, my boy. Your father was a very important man. He had many friends. Have you stopped to think that even now some of them may be trying to clear his name?"

Aahmes brightened at the thought. His father had indeed had many friends. Perhaps . . . "Yes, Master, I'll go home," he agreed. He rose and walked to the door. Outside he heard the sounds of the other boys at play, as carefree as he had been only yesterday. It seemed like ages ago. He turned to look once more at the place where he had sat for so many years.

The old teacher followed him to the doorway, and as he started down the steps, called out, "Horus go with thee and protect thee . . . " The rest of his words were lost amid the babble of voices outside. The students fell silent and backed away from Aahmes as he passed, then continued their game of leap-frog as soon as he had moved out of the courtyard into the street beyond.

He was in no hurry to go home. The earlier he arrived, the sooner he would have to explain why he had left before school was over. He kicked a stone aimlessly along in front of him.

He did not look up from the ground until, as he neared the entrance to his house, he heard someone call his name. Hemon was standing in the doorway beckoning to him. "Oh, master, have you not heard the news?" the steward said, hurrying him inside.

Heard the news? What else could have happened?

"What news, Hemon?"

"Your brother, Master Khepri. The Pharaoh's police came here this morning and placed him under arrest!"

# ESCAPE

Aahmes was too shocked to speak as Hemon recited the details of his brother's arrest. Khepri had somehow managed to slip out of Thebes with his father's body and carry it into the desert. But on his return he had been arrested by the Pharaoh's police.

How had they known? The Great One himself, of course. It was said that he travelled across the sky in the disguise of a falcon. He saw everywhere, knew everything. Nobody could keep secrets from him. Poor Khepri knew this but had taken the risk anyway. Duty to family had outweighed obedience to the Pharaoh. Aahmes sank dejectedly onto a pile of cushions.

"The police?" he asked, unbelievingly.

"Yes, master. Nubians. May the God Seth take them."

"But Hemon, what am I to do now? Is there anything I can do to help Khepri?"

"No, master. You must pretend you know nothing of

what has happened. The Pharaoh sees everywhere and punishes all those who oppose his will. You must do nothing to arouse suspicion against yourself — or against the household," he added.

"But he's my brother," Aahmes protested.

"And that is why he's in trouble, master — because he's your father's son. But you have nothing to fear. I will see to all your wishes."

"Thank you, Hemon, I'm sure you will. I just don't know what to do with myself. I've already been asked to stay away from school."

"Ah" — a peculiar smile played over the features of the steward — "the story of your father is known even there."

"The lies about my father, you mean," retorted the boy heatedly.

"Of course, master. There is no truth in the charges. Horem-heb would not do anything to cause harm to the Great One. In time the Gods will clear him of all blame."

Aahmes looked puzzled. "But Hemon, if he is innocent, and the Pharaoh knows everything, why was he slain?" He wished he had asked such questions of Old Senmut.

"Ah, master, the ways of the world are very strange. Remember, the Gods take many away to the Celestial Fields to reward them for their good services."

"Yes, but Khepri and I are left to suffer . . . "

"Master, time will correct all. People forget such scandals in a surprisingly short time. Believe me, you will see. By the time the next Harvest Season is upon us, no one will bother to speak of it any more."

"Do you really think so? And Khepri?"

"After all, he is not guilty of such a serious crime," Hemon reassured him. "He did defy the Pharaoh, but he was acting as a son should act. The Great One may be merciful."

Aahmes smiled. Perhaps the steward, who seemed to know so much about life, was right after all. If so, it might turn out that at least he and Khepri would be left undisturbed to tend the lands of their father. Their hopes for careers in the army had been dashed, but he supposed that they would be quite well off as farmers — even wealthy. Together they could take charge of running the estate. "But Hemon, what am I to do for now?" he asked again. "Isn't there some way I can help Khepri?"

"I will send a servant to find out what he can. I promise nothing, but we might at least discover if Khepri is all right or if he is in need of anything in prison."

"Khepri?" Aahmes gave Hemon a stern look.

"*Master* Khepri, I meant." The head steward blinked and offered his oily smile. "I fear the incidents of the past two days have affected us all," he went on smoothly. "Even to forgetting our places."

Aahmes accepted this, but decided he had better grow accustomed to giving orders rather than asking advice. "Go and see what can be learned," he commanded.

"Young master, I will send someone at once." The steward bowed deeply and left the room. Something in the back of Aahmes' mind warned him not to trust the man. But he seemed to have little choice. If he sent Hemon away, how would he be able to control all the servants and slaves? They could be unruly and sullen when not kept in their place, especially the foreign slaves. They might even become dangerous. He began to wish he had paid more attention to the management of the household. It could be months before Khepri was released — at least until the Pharaoh returned from Libya — and he would be required to make decisions in the meantime.

At the moment there was little he could do but take Hemon's word for everything. Anyway, the head steward had always seemed honest enough, if not particularly likable. Perhaps it was just his appearance that was against him: his massive forehead and moist, snake-like eyes, with hardly any eyebrows. Those features were certainly not reassuring.

Aahmes stood up and began pacing about the room. It was a beautiful room, with four tall lotus pillars supporting the roof from within. The floor was lower in the centre, so that guests could easily see any entertainment offered there. The walls were painted a pale green so that nothing detracted from the magnificent pillars.

From somewhere in the house he heard a door opening and closing. That was probably the servant Hemon had sent to find out about Khepri. Strange, though — it sounded like the garden door. The way from the front entrance would have been faster. True, the servants seldom used it, but this was no ordinary task. He was anxious to hear news of his brother and thought the quickest possible means should have been employed. Still, he must be careful not to question the chief steward's judgement regarding the details of carrying out his orders; his father had often told him that interference in small matters was the way to undermine authority so that in time the slaves would obey no one. Aahmes was determined to be the best master possible, and to support those set in authority over others. He would learn all there was to know about the estate, and Khepri would be proud of him when he found everything running smoothly upon his return.

But what was that sound? It had come from the hallway. He strode across the room and pulled aside the heavy curtain that fell from ceiling to floor. "Who is there?" he demanded. "Who sneaks around to hear things not intended for his ears?"

A shadow moved away from the wall, but for a moment he could not see who it was. Then it moved closer to him, and in the dim light he saw the Syrian slave girl Anath-herte. As always, Aahmes was struck by her beauty, and he found his anger softening. What would become of his resolve to rule over the entire household, though, if the servants discovered he had favourites among them? He tried to be stern. "Is that you, Anath-herte? What are you doing sneaking about like a jackal in the night?"

The girl glided forward noiselessly and fell to the floor before him, pressing her forehead against his feet. "Oh please, master, keep your voice low," she whispered, glancing behind her in terror.

"Stop this nonsense," he commanded, lowering his voice a little. "What is it, Anath-herte? What's the matter?"

"I — I was working in the other room just now when Hemon came by. He told Ran, the son of Taui, to sneak out the back way and fetch the Nubians to arrest you, master."

Aahmes stepped back, drawing his foot away from her. "Arrest me? Don't be silly. Why would they want to arrest me?"

"Hemon told Ran to say that you had helped your brother Khepri when he buried your father."

Aahmes stood perfectly still, stunned. Could Anath-herte be telling the truth? Were his deep suspicions and feelings concerning Hemon to be more trusted after all than his knowledge of the man's past service? He took his uncertainty out on the slave.

"You are a silly girl, Anath-herte. You should be beaten for what you have said. Why would Hemon want to have me arrested? I'm the only remaining son of Horem-heb. How could the estates be managed without me?"

"Master, he plans to run them for himself, as he has done since the death of your mother."

"You mean he's been stealing from us?"

"I — I don't know, master."

"Of course you don't. Can you read or write?" he asked, superior because of his training as a scribe.

"No, master. But I have heard him whispering to the food suppliers, and I do not think he is to be trusted."

"But how would he benefit if I were arrested?"

"I'm — I'm not certain, master." She hesitated, then rushed on. "I suppose if you were taken away he'd be able to run the whole estate, with no one to bother him. He could steal everything for himself then. And besides," she added, "he thinks the Pharaoh will reward him for having you imprisoned."

Aahmes frowned. He did not know what to do, what to think, whom to believe. Was managing the estate going to bring him a series of seemingly insoluble problems? If so, he was neither trained nor equipped for the job.

"I don't believe you," he snapped. "Don't you know that slaves who spread lies are whipped?"

"Yes, master. If I'm wrong, I'll be beaten at your

order. And if Hemon finds out I have spoken to you, he will have me whipped himself. A slave never wins in either event."

Well, she certainly spoke the truth, Aahmes had to admit. She was risking a severe punishment, no matter what. "Why do you tell me this then?" he asked, speaking more kindly this time.

"I — feel sorry for you, master. And for Khepri . . . Master Khepri."

"Khepri?"

"If you are imprisoned, there will be no hope of his being freed."

That was probably true too. The girl seemed to have more sense than most slaves. Suppose the rest of what she had said were also true? Would it not be wise for him to leave this house immediately? But where would he go? He had no friends, it appeared, none at all — except for this slave, perhaps. And how could she help?

As he stood there pondering, she said, "Please, master, there is not much time. Ran will be back any moment with the police."

What was he to do? Be frightened away from his own home by the foolish tales of a slave? Or be driven away by the wicked schemes of the head steward? He was hopelessly confused, and yet he was beginning to trust Anath-herte more than the crafty Hemon. Suppose the steward really had been stealing from the estate? He might fear discovery, and that would account for his

betrayal.

Suddenly Aahmes made up his mind. He reached down and touched Anath-herte on the shoulder. "Thank you. I believe your story. Now hurry back before you are discovered and beaten for your pains. I'll not forget what you have done for me, Anath-herte."

"Yes, master." She rose to her feet and looked into his eyes for a moment. "Here, take this," she said. "It is an *ankh,* the Eye of Horus. It will protect you." From her own neck she slipped a papyrus cord on which hung the hieroglyph for *life.* The cross-shaped metal symbol was probably her only possession.

Aahmes did not know what to say. He moved back to the entryway and peered out to see if they had been overheard. There he paused and turned to thank her, but she had already disappeared. Just as he was opening the gate, he looked out and saw Ran leading four Nubian policemen around to the back of the building. Fortunately none of them saw Aahmes. He slipped across the road and down the next street. In no time at all, he knew, the alarm would be out for him, and this side of the Nile would be thoroughly searched. Somehow, he must cross the river.

Once on the other side, he would have to reach the Great One and make him believe the truth. This desperate plan meant swimming the river, crossing the desert beyond and somehow reaching the Libyan frontier. He had no idea how he would ever accomplish all that, but at least he had to try. It was better than letting the Nubian police put him in prison where he would be no use to anyone.

At the water's edge, Aahmes paused. Fortunately the river had begun to recede, and he was a fairly good swimmer. He had no money to rent a boat and would not have risked it anyway. The owner of the boat would be sure to tell the police. Quietly he slid into the water.

When he finally reached the other side, he found that he had drifted quite far north. That was good, he thought. At least he was closer to the Libyan frontier, although how far away it still was he had not the least idea.

He set off across the patchwork of small square fields, threading his way among the canals that were exactly like those on his own side of the Nile. Finally he left behind the area that the river had flooded. All he could see before him was the desert and the cloudless blue sky above.

It would not be long, Aahmes realized, before the Nubian police discovered that he had crossed the river. They would alert the desert police, and the dark-skinned Sudanese would soon be on his trail. He was well aware of their reputation for tracking fugitives across the sand and rock of the desert. Not even waiting for his clothing to dry in the heat of the blazing sun, the boy set off at a run towards the distant horizon.

# THE EYE OF HORUS

Fortunately, Aahmes had worn his sandals. Otherwise the rocky surface would have cut his feet to ribbons. He ran as fast as he could, intending to put as much distance as possible between himself and the river. There were too many inhabitants along the banks, too many curious people who might ask questions he dared not answer.

His plan, insofar as he had one, was to make his way as far as he could into the desert, hoping that he might meet a caravan on its way to the Libyan frontier, where the Great One was. His hope was a slim one at best, but in his panic he could think of nothing better.

Hemon would surely have guessed his intentions, and by this time the Nubian police would be scouring the shoreline. Possibly the steward had also found out that Anath-herte had given the warning. If so, she would be in serious trouble. There was nothing Aahmes could do to help her, though, except reach the Great One and make him believe his story.

Maybe the police would hire a boat to pursue him across the Nile — someone was almost certain to have noticed him while he was swimming. And once across, they would no doubt ask the Sudanese trackers for help. Even now he might meet one of the desert squads at any moment, and if he did, they would undoubtedly take him to their nearest outpost, no matter what he told them. Somehow he must avoid that. They would keep him until they had checked his story, and only Horus knew how long that would take.

Aahmes ran on, occasionally darting glances over his shoulder. But he saw no one. He almost wished he would, for he was beginning to feel lonely. If only his friend Kames were with him! Friend? For a moment he had forgotten his fight with his former companion, but now the bitter memory came rushing back to him.

The desert *was* a lonely place. He wished that he and Khepri had escaped together. His brother would make a fine comrade, for he was always making jokes, always finding something to laugh about in every situation. Aahmes felt sorry that he had not awakened in time to go with his older brother. He could have helped him in the burial of their father. They would have finished sooner and his brother might not have been caught. Or at least they would have been arrested and imprisoned together.

He wondered how Khepri was and how he was being

treated. He had many friends in the army; perhaps they would see to it that he received food and other comforts. But suppose they were no better than Aahmes' own friends were? He shrugged that off. Soldiers who had fought together and shared the same dangers were closer than other companions. They would stand by him.

Soon he would be leaving the rocky rim of the desert and entering the sandy area. He paused to catch his breath and noted that the line where desert and sky met seemed to be just as far away as ever. He walked out into the sand, feeling it trickle down between his toes and out the sides of his sandals with each step.

The wind had swept the sand into huge dunes here, and the going was slower. He had to climb each mound, frequently sliding back almost as far as he had clambered up, then skidding down the other side, trying his best to remain upright as his feet sank into the shifting sand. All the while his mind kept worrying away at his problem.

If he reached the frontier while the Great One was still there, he might be able to see him and tell his story. If the Pharaoh knew everything, he would certainly right the wrong that had been done to Horem-heb and Khepri. Was it not his duty to maintain law and order in the land? And how could that be done without justice?

As Aahmes looked back, he could no longer see the river. All about him was dry hot sand. He was growing tired and beginning to wish he had brought some food along, and drink. Especially drink.

He was terribly thirsty, but did not dare turn back to the river. He was no longer even certain where it was. Each sand dune looked like the one he had just climbed and he had slipped and fallen so many times that he could easily have got turned around. He had no choice but to keep going and hope for the best. Perhaps he would be lucky and find some food and water.

But would he be lucky enough to avoid the dreaded Bedouin tribes that lived in the desert? To find an Egyptian-led caravan? To elude the desert police? Nothing in his life had prepared him for a predicament like this. He had always just accepted his position in life, his father's importance, his family's wealth and estates. But in the middle of the desert, none of these meant anything. What was that saying he had copied out so many times at the Temple of Life? Something about a wise man preparing during good times for the misfortune that might befall him. Well, he had written it out many times, but that didn't mean he had heeded it. Now here he was — alone, afraid and without provisions.

Suddenly a pleasant thought struck him. If Khepri had been arrested on his way back from the desert, that meant that their father had already been buried. Not as he deserved, of course, in a real tomb, but still buried. Aahmes wondered if all the prayers were required so long as the body was properly cared for.

At least now Horem-heb could be judged. Osiris would know his heart was pure. When it was weighed against the feather of truth, Horem-heb would be found innocent and sent on to the Celestial Fields. Perhaps he was even now gliding down the Nile with his wife, Nephthys.

The boy stumbled on, mechanically climbing one sand dune after another, until he almost blundered into a desert patrol. What saved him was that his eye happened to catch a movement over the rise ahead of him. He dropped to his stomach and burrowed down into the sand. He didn't know what he had seen, wasn't even certain he had seen anything, but he lay perfectly still for some time. At last he crawled cautiously to the top of the rise.

A Sudanese foot patrol was marching silently past, their black skins dusty. Over their shoulders they carried long spears whose points glinted in the sun. They were apparently a regular patrol heading towards the river after a long march across the sandy hills. Surely they could not be searching for him already.

Aahmes huddled against the rise until they were out of sight, then leaped to his feet and began to run as fast as he could, struggling desperately to maintain his footing in the trackless sand.

# LOST!

Aahmes kept on running until long after he was sure that the patrol was really gone. Sharp stones cut his feet in spite of his sandals, and the hot sun beat down mercilessly on his bare head. His breath came in short gasps. At last, unable to go farther, he collapsed onto the sand.

There he lay, trying to regain control of his breathing and to think clearly about his situation. No doubt the Sudanese would eventually be sent out to track him down. They were accustomed to living and travelling in the desert. Sometimes they even used chariots and hunting dogs. What chance would he have of avoiding capture against such odds?

But he must reach the Pharaoh. Surely the Great One would listen to his explanation. What he could not understand, though, was why a God would not know the truth without being told.

For some time Aahmes remained where he was on

the sand. The hot sun began to make him feel very drowsy and he forgot the Sudanese and the problems that plagued him. His memory drifted back to the happy days when his mother, Nephthys, was alive — before she had gone to the Field of Rushes and the Field of Offerings. If Horem-heb had been judged and found innocent by Osiris, he would be with her now. Perhaps someday the whole family would be reunited there. That happy thought lulled his tired body to the verge of sleep.

He woke with a start. For a moment he didn't know where he was, but then all the bitter memories came flooding back. What was he to do?

It would be a simple matter just to wait to be caught. If he were killed, he would have nothing more to worry about. But Khepri — what would become of him? If the Great One ordered Khepri's execution for disobeying orders, would he be properly buried? No, of course not. He would be thrown to the crocodiles. So the family would not be reunited after all in the land where the Sweet Breezes of the North Wind would cool them forever and waft their boats along the sacred Nile.

He was not worried about facing and being judged by the Devourer. None of his family needed to fear that; they were all innocent of any crime. His father had served the Pharaoh throughout his life and would continue to do so in the next world. Was there not an understanding that the safety of Egypt depended upon caring for and preserving the bodies and memories of great men, who would then be able to strengthen and bestow blessings upon the Two Lands?

But the burial of Horem-heb must have been a hurried affair, without the proper prayers being said. Khepri had stolen the body to save it from mutilation, for unless the body was kept whole there was no future life. He wished he knew more about the world of the Gods. Why had he not listened more closely to Old Senmut's explanations?

Aahmes stood up, feeling somewhat refreshed and ready to go on. But as he looked about him, he realized that he was hopelessly lost. He had no idea which direction he had come from, or where he should go. All he could see were scattered rocks and sand dunes. The whole landscape looked the same. He turned, trying to remember which way the patrol had gone, but he was uncertain even of that. He could easily end up following in their very footsteps without knowing it.

The rocks would give him no clue of course, as they were too hard to show tracks. As for the sand, any traces left there were quickly erased by the wind. So Aahmes started forward blindly. Perhaps he could at least find a sheltered spot.

The afternoon sun beat down on his head — Horus on his daily chariot ride over the Two Lands. When night came the God would plunge into the underworld, to reappear at dawn, once again bringing light and heat to Egypt. Aahmes would welcome the coolness of the evening, though later on, he knew, he would begin to feel cold.

But now the sun looked like a fiery red ball. It seared Aahmes' flesh and glared into his eyes, practically blinding him. Could the God not be merciful, he wondered, and limit his shining might? After all, Horus himself had once avenged his father's death on the murderer Seth, his own brother. While their mother Isis gathered up the pieces to sew her husband together again, Horus had pursued Seth into the desert and killed him.

Wearily Aahmes clambered up another sand dune. On top was a large rock with a lizard resting under it. Even the creatures of the desert have more sense than to remain out in the sun, he thought. Too bad the rock isn't big enough to offer me protection too. There was nothing to do but go on.

The hawk-headed God's rays covered almost every inch of the vast plateau that now stretched before him. More slowly this time, Aahmes picked up his weary feet and trudged on through the sand, vainly searching the horizon for an oasis that would provide shelter for the night, water to drink, and dates to eat.

He was beginning to lose hope. How long could he continue? Thirst was becoming a serious problem now. And he was hungry too. If only he had brought along some food and water! He thought of the delicious meal that was probably being prepared at this very moment in the kitchens of his home.

That reminded him of Hemon. If he ever reached the Great One, he would tell him about the head steward too. And the Pharaoh, who hated evil, would have him punished in some fitting way.

Aahmes' lips were parched, and his tongue felt like a leather sandal in his mouth. He tried to keep moving straight ahead, but no matter how hard he concentrated, he seemed to be weaving from side to side.

The hot eye of Horus . . . His head swam dizzily. Why had the God turned against him? What had he or his family ever done to earn such ill will? Had they forgotten to honour him in some way? Had they neglected the sacrifices? Aahmes tried to remember if he had said or done anything, anything at all that might have offended the falcon-headed God. But he could think of nothing. Indeed, he could scarcely recall his own name.

Suppose the Pharaoh appeared before him at this moment? What would he think, except that every member of Horem-heb's family must be crazy? Aahmes would not be able to explain his mission. His tongue was too swollen for speaking now, and his brain was scarcely functioning at all.

Did that mean he was going to die? He stumbled clumsily over a rock that he had not even seen. With each step his legs felt heavier. If only he could find an oasis — even a small one with two or three palms under which he could lie and rest. Ahead loomed another dune like a mountain to be climbed. Would he reach the top of this one? If he did, would it really make any difference? How many more lay beyond? Would he go on struggling over one dune after another until death finally came to set him free? It would be a death without family and without prayers or proper burial — a death like that of his father.

He trudged on resolutely, only to trip and fall flat on his back. Get up, an inner voice seemed to tell him. Slowly he rolled over onto his stomach and began to crawl forward. Every time he moved a hand or a knee, sand flooded the hollow he had created.

He struggled to the top of the next dune, eyes shut against the glare of the setting sun. He tumbled over the edge and rolled down into yet another rock-strewn valley, his arms and knees scraped and bleeding. He lay looking straight into the fiery eye of Horus. I must roll over and continue, as a good soldier would, he thought. Always keep moving, his father had told him. But his limbs refused to obey.

The sun seemed to grow larger and nearer. Horus was coming right down on top of him, he thought. He tried to force his eyes open, to face the God without fear. But even as he did so, his head fell back and he lost consciousness.

# AND FOUND

"Wake up, child!"

Aahmes looked up through half-closed lids. He was lying on his back, and at first he could distinguish nothing. Perhaps Horus had taken his sight away from him for defying the Great One. Then his eyes began focusing and he saw that he was inside a tent. Was this what it was like to be dead, or was he still among the living? He was uncertain, for he had no feeling in his limbs.

He let his eyes roam until they finally rested on the source of the voice. "Wake up, I say," it ordered him again.

Beside the bed, with his hands on his hips, stood a magnificent figure wearing a *nems* on his head and carrying the staff of office of a troop captain. An Egyptian soldier! Thank Horus, Aahmes thought.

But then he remembered that he was a fugitive. Suppose the word had spread? Perhaps he had been found by one of the regular desert patrols. Well, at least he had tried. He had done all he could.

"Look, he's coming to," another voice said, and Aahmes turned his head to see a servant bending over him, applying a cooling cloth to his forehead. The boy struggled to a sitting position and the cloth dropped to his chest.

"Where am I?" he asked.

"In the caravan of Tety the Handsome," the servant answered. "What were you doing wandering across the desert by yourself? Don't you know you might have died? Here, drink this," he commanded, handing the boy a cup of strong broth. Aahmes drank it eagerly. He felt its warmth surge through his body, and with it, his strength began to return. He finished drinking, but clung to the cup while he tried to think of some acceptable explanation for his wandering in the desert. At least these people did not appear to know he was wanted by the Pharaoh's police. Finally he answered, "I wandered too far from home. I was lost and couldn't find my way back."

"Your parents will certainly be worried about you," answered the officer identified as Tety. "And we have no way of letting them know where you are. We have to cross to the Libyan frontier, and I have only one ᶜ on of forty men to guard an entire caravan."

So there was no turning back. Good. That meant Tety might not learn his real identity. But Aahmes realized that he had to appear concerned, like a lost boy who really wanted to return home. "What can I do?" he moaned.

"Now, don't worry," the officer answered soothingly. "As soon as we reach the frontier, we'll send word back that you're safe and sound. Perhaps we'll meet a caravan returning to your home. Where are you from?"

"Luxor, my lord."

"Ah, yes. I've been there many times. You don't appear to be a peasant's son. What is your name and who is your father?"

Aahmes hesitated for only a moment before answering. "I am Kames, son of Apepa. My father is a scribe in the tax department." At least he could borrow the name and family of his former friend. Kames owed him that much for the unkind and untrue things he'd said about his father.

"Kames? Well, welcome to my caravan then, Kames, son of Apepa. I've been put in charge of an army of sheep and goats that are being sent to reinforce the rest of the herds on the frontier." The soldier laughed. "They're at least as bright as some of the men I've commanded. Perhaps when you're feeling better, you'll become my deputy assistant and take your place at the head of a platoon."

"You mean work with the animals?"

"That's it. All men work with animals, except that some have four legs while others have only two." Tety laughed again.

"I can begin right away, my lord."

"There's no rush. We don't want you to collapse again."

Aahmes leaped to his feet. "No, really. I'm ready now. Perhaps we should be moving immediately." He was anxious to put as much distance between himself and Luxor as possible. The officer looked at him sharply, and the boy added quickly, "It cannot be good to remain in one place too long when there are Bedouins about."

"That's true enough," agreed Tety. He turned to his servant. "Sa-Mentu, give the order that we are to proceed at once."

The servant bowed and left the tent. Aahmes moved to the entrance and looked out. All around were the sights and sounds of a desert caravan. Merchants were mounting their mules. Protesting sheep and noisy goats were being led off. There were a few horses about, and he noticed two chariots stationed outside the tent.

"You were lucky we stumbled across you," Tety said.

"Yes, my lord. I would have been dead if you hadn't."

"Well," the handsome warrior admitted, "that's probably true. At least saving your skin gives some meaning to our journey. I don't enjoy escorting stupid animals and merchants back and forth across this Seth-invented desert. It's unfit for man or beast."

"Don't you like being a soldier for the Great One?" Aahmes asked in surprise.

"I enjoy the fighting," Tety replied. "It's exciting and I'm good at it. But anyone can chase animals. And I'm afraid I'm not very diplomatic when it comes to dealing with these merchants."

Aahmes laughed. The officer showed a typical military attitude, seeing no purpose in anything but marching and fighting. Someday he would be just the same, he told himself, if his mission succeeded. Tety turned him over to one of his men, who showed him a herd of goats and gave him a stick to drive them forward with.

The caravan was obviously carrying food and other necessities to the army on the frontier; so they would be travelling directly to where the Pharaoh was. It might be possible, once there, for Aahmes to sneak in and see the Great One. He might even get to him more easily than he could at the regular court.

Aahmes wished he could tell Tety his real name and explain his mission. He liked the soldier, who seemed very much like his brother — only older and more experienced. Perhaps Tety would be able to help him? But no. If the commander knew who he really was, it would be his duty to have him placed under arrest. What happened to him after he had spoken to the Great One did not matter, but for now he had to remain free.

The caravan marched until darkness fell, since Tety was anxious to reach the frontier and the fighting at the earliest possible moment. Aahmes was excited at that prospect too, but he was not sorry when they finally made camp for the night. He was given a good meal of goat flesh and a cloak to cover himself with for the night. Since he had become a shepherd, it was his duty to stay with the herds and make sure that none of the animals wandered off or were stolen by the Bedouins who came and went as quietly as birds along the Nile.

The men sat around the fire trading stories of their adventures, as soldiers always do. There was nothing Aahmes would have enjoyed more than listening to them, but when he tried to settle the animals near enough to the fire so that he could hear snatches of their conversation, the men told him that the smell of the goats, together with the warmth from the fire, was too much for even the bravest of them.

Reluctantly Aahmes moved the herd to the very edge of the camp and settled them there for the night. He lay on the ground near them, but found it difficult to sleep because a young goat that had taken to following him around insisted on lying with its head on his neck. Every so often it would lick the boy's face and startle him. But finally, in spite of the kid and the cold night air that blew through his cloak, he drifted off into a dream about being a soldier for the Pharaoh.

The next time he was awakened by the goat nudging against him, everything was completely dark. Overhead the stars shone brightly, each twinkling in the exact spot where it had been set by the God of Creation, Ptah. Aahmes smiled in contentment, for they seemed like beacons of hope to guide him to his destination. He knew, of course, that every one of them was a separate God, and tonight he thought they were trying to signal him not to give up hope. He was determined to follow their advice.

Glancing over towards the fire, he noticed that everyone had gone to bed. Only a few burning embers glowed in the darkness, though Aahmes knew it must still be a long time before dawn. He rolled over, pulling the cloak more closely around him, only to have his face licked again by the young goat.

Suddenly a sound caught his ear. At first he didn't know what it was. He lay perfectly still, listening carefully, until it came again. He noticed that the goats seemed disturbed. A few of them had risen to their feet and were milling about. A tail swept across his face.

Surely there was no cause for alarm — Tety had positioned guards around the entire camp. But this thought did not completely reassure Aahmes, since at that moment he heard the sound of someone creeping past the goat herd. Perhaps one of Tety's men had been looking for him, but had given up and gone back towards the camp. What could it mean? If someone wanted him, why not just call? Maybe somebody had, while he was asleep, and because Kames was not his real name, he hadn't paid any attention.

As these thoughts ran through his mind, Aahmes heard and saw several other mysterious figures stealing past the herd. Why didn't the animals make more of a fuss? he wondered. Suddenly the answer came to him. Because, he told himself, these men were Bedouins, who were said to smell more like goats than goats did themselves. Well, what did that mean? It meant, he concluded, that the caravan was being attacked!

But where were the guards? Had they not heard the stealthy movements? Perhaps they had already been killed. If so, the attackers would now be moving through the camp in large numbers to murder the rest of the caravan as they slept.

Aahmes lay there, stiff with fright, painfully aware that any movement would give him away. The Bedouins had come like this for only one reason: they intended to butcher the whole caravan! What should he do? There was still time to crawl away from the camp, reach the desert and run for his life, he told himself. He tried to force himself to believe that his own safety and his mission were more important than anything else, since his whole family depended on him. But he knew he could not leave Egyptians to be slaughtered in their sleep. Somehow he had to reach Tety and alert him to what was happening. Tety would believe him. Cautiously Aahmes began to crawl through the herd of goats, using the animals to conceal himself. But he was hampered by his companion, who accompanied him and licked his face every time he paused along the way.

He tried pushing the kid away, but it was persistent. Occasionally it bleated softly, and now that he was beyond the herd, it could easily draw attention to his exposed position. He continued forward on his hands and knees, hoping that if he were spotted he would be mistaken for a goat.

At last he came within sight of Tety's tent. It was not far now, but the rest of his journey was across open ground, and all of a sudden the moon seemed unusually bright. With luck, one quick dash should carry him there and inside, he thought. He rose soundlessly to his feet, and as he did so, he spotted the sleeping form of a man directly in front of him. He dropped to his knees again and placed his hand on the ground beside the figure. His fingers came up sticky with blood. In the light of the moon he noticed that the man was an Egyptian soldier — with a terrible slash across his throat. He must have been one of the guards set out to prevent just such an attack.

Perhaps the Bedouins had already killed Tety, in which case his warning would be useless. The whole camp could be dead by now, he told himself. If he entered the tent, he would probably get himself killed. One of the attackers might even now be waiting inside for him. Should he continue or go back while there might still be time for him to escape?

Aahmes paused, uncertain which was the wiser course to follow.

# A WARNING

Aahmes knew fear, real paralysing fear. What should he do? The man's throat had been cut only a short time before; in the light of the moon he could see blood still oozing from the wound. Were the Bedouins even now completing their task by murdering Tety?

He wanted to run. But he reminded himself that he was the son of a soldier, and that his own people were involved. He could not turn and flee when other Egyptians needed him. But how could he raise the alarm? Even if he crossed the camp and managed to reach the other sleeping soldiers, they might not believe him. Somehow he had to reach the commander's tent, waken him if it was not already too late, and tell him what was happening.

Aahmes forced himself to stretch out his hand and draw the guard's sword from its sheath. At least now he had a weapon with which to strike back if he were attacked. On his hands and knees, he backed away from the dead soldier. When he was far enough into the shadows of the palm tree, he stood up and ran around to the other side of the tent, so as to approach from the rear.

There was no sound in the camp, which probably meant that only the guards had been dealt with, that the Bedouins had not yet reached the sleeping recruits. Or maybe they had all been slaughtered already. Aahmes stood still for a moment in the shadow of the tent, then plunged the sword into the heavy fabric, sawing methodically up and down to cut a hole big enough to let him through. He did it as quietly as possible, but the ripping sound seemed loud enough to him to be heard throughout the whole camp. When the tear was large enough, he wriggled through, sword first, as he knew was the proper way for a soldier.

None of the moon's bright illumination penetrated the tent, and inside it was pitch dark. Where was Tety likely to sleep?

Aahmes remembered that this was the tent in which he had regained consciousness after being found in the desert. Probably he had been laid on the captain's bed. If that were so, it was likely that it had been in its regular position, even though the caravan had stopped for only a short rest. Surely he should be able to find it, even without light.

Cautiously he moved forward, stumbling once over a box of some sort and then bumping into the pole that supported the tent. He should be close to the bed now, he thought. Falling to his hands and knees, he began to crawl forward. If Tety were still alive, it would not do to trip and fall over him, raising an alarm so that the Bedouins would hear and come to finish their work.

He wondered if it would be difficult to waken the captain. Or was he a light sleeper, as a good soldier should be? Carefully Aahmes reached out a hand. At that moment his arm was seized in a powerful grip, and he found himself being pulled forward as if he weighed no more than a feather. Then he felt himself being crushed against a powerful chest. The breath was forced from his lungs, and he was unable even to cry out.

Whoever held him made no sound. It might be a Bedouin sent to kill the captain. Or possibly it was the servant. But would he not be likely to raise an alarm?

Then he heard a voice mutter, "They certainly sent a small one to murder me."

It was Tety! "Te — ty," gasped Aahmes. The pressure on his chest relaxed, and he was released and rolled over onto the ground. He gulped for air and found the blade of a sword across his stomach.

"Who speaks my name in the dark?" demanded the officer.

Without thinking, the boy answered, "It is I, Aahmes, son of Horem-heb."

"Son of a traitor, just as I supposed," the other returned.

So he had suspected the truth. "Oh, no, Tety. My father was no traitor."

"Then why has his son run away into the desert? And why does he travel under a false name?"

"To try to reach the Great One and tell him the truth. I was afraid that you would send me back to Luxor, that's why I didn't tell you my real name."

"And how did you think creeping around the camp and ripping your way into my tent in the middle of the night would help you in your quest?"

"That's not why I'm here. I came to warn you. We're under attack by a group of Bedouins. They've broken into the camp and have already murdered some of your guards."

"How do you know all this?"

"I was awakened a short while ago and heard them moving about. I came to tell you and found that the man outside your tent had been killed."

Tety remained silent for a few moments. "Is this true?" he asked sternly.

"By Horus, who brought me safely to your caravan, it is," the boy swore.

"Then there is little time to lose. We can expect some unwelcome visitors very shortly. Are you armed?"

"Yes, my lord. I took the sword from your murdered guard."

"That was good thinking. Do you know how to use it?"

"Yes. My father is — was a Commander of the Shock Troops."

"Yes, I knew your father. In fact, I served under him at one time earlier in my career. But isn't there an older son in your family? I seem to recall — "

"Yes. His name is Khepri. He's been placed under arrest."

"Oh. Well, we can discuss that later — if we survive. Unless my ears deceive me, our visitors will soon be here."

The soldier rose to his feet, and with the boy standing slightly behind him, turned to face the entrance. A shaft of moonlight cut across in front of them as a lone figure slipped stealthily into the tent.

# THE ATTACK

Aahmes stood tall and straight beside Tety, both of them armed with swords. The flaps parted again, admitting the bright desert moonlight and another shadowy form. In the brief shaft of light, Aahmes, whose eyes were by now accustomed to the dark, noticed that Tety had not undressed to sleep. His admiration for the captain increased even more. Another pair of dark figures slipped in and glided to either side, away from the entrance. At the same time, a tearing sound came from behind them. Some of the attackers were tearing their way into the tent, just as Aahmes had done.

What had become of the soldiers? Had all their throats been cut? And the other men — the merchants in the caravan — had all of them died without waking? Or was that being attended to right now?

Tety remained perfectly still, not wanting the Bedouins to know he was awake. Stealthy sounds indicated movement towards the bed. The tearing continued, then stopped abruptly.

Suddenly several of the men who had entered the tent lunged towards the bed and buried their knives into what they assumed to be the sleeping captain. As they did so, Tety let out a mighty shout and threw himself on top of them, lashing out with his sword. That should certainly have awakened the rest of the camp, Aahmes thought.

The tent flaps parted again and two more figures entered. Tety leaped forward, striking out again with all his strength. As he did so, Aahmes glanced back and saw someone slip in through a gaping hole in the side of the tent. He stood there uncertainly. Tety's back was turned. The newcomer looked around, but missed Aahmes in the darkness. He drew his dagger and prepared to join the scuffle in front of him.

Slowly he advanced on Tety's back. Aahmes was terrified, but saw that he would have to act. He stepped up and attacked the intruder. The man emitted a long low moan, then he spun around and seized the boy. But even as he did so, life went out of him and he sank slowly to his knees, his weight crushing Aahmes to the ground.

The boy tried to struggle free, but the man was too heavy. The sound of fighting continued. Aahmes heard someone grunt and go down near him. He struggled again and this time managed to pull himself to a sitting position.

Just then another Bedouin entered the tent. There was no time to lose. With a mighty heave that took all his strength, Aahmes managed to free himself completely. He felt around in the darkness and finally located his sword.

He tripped over something bulky on the ground. It had to be a body, but he didn't stop to investigate. He struggled to his feet once more and over to where the commander was fighting so magnificently.

As he approached, Tety swung around, raising his sword again. But he stopped abruptly. "Is that you, Aahmes?"

"Yes, my lord. Let me help."

"You've already done that. I saw what you did to our friend who entered from the side." He turned quickly to face another attacker.

Aahmes took his place by Tety's side. The captain must be tiring, he thought. How long could even an Egyptian go on fighting against such odds?

He stopped thinking at that moment as he faced another Bedouin with a knife. Aahmes caught the curved blade on the hilt of his straight sword, just as his father had taught him to, and pushed back. The man was caught by surprise and lost his footing. He tripped and fell backwards. Leaping forward, Aahmes struck him on the arm with the edge of the sword. The intruder shrieked, then turned tail and ran from the tent.

Unfortunately his place was taken by two more, who

both advanced on the boy. Springing to the side of his young friend, Tety struck one of the Bedouins on the side of the head. The man fell heavily, and in a moment the second man likewise succumbed to a slashing blow.

Tety and Aahmes retreated to the back of the tent to catch their breath during the momentary respite. Aahmes felt huge drops of sweat rolling down his back. He sank onto the cushions to rest.

Tety smiled down at him. "It's easy to see you're the son of a soldier, my brave young friend."

"They'll keep on coming, won't they, Tety?"

"Oh, yes. They'll be back. And very soon, I should judge. That's typical of their methods. Without all the animals and merchants we were escorting, we could have moved much faster and avoided danger. Bedouins don't attack unless they catch you at a disadvantage. It's really the herds of animals they're after anyway. I even doubled the guard tonight, just to be on the safe side." He swept his sleeve across his forehead, wiping away beads of perspiration. "It still wasn't enough," he continued. "I should have remained awake myself."

"But you can't blame yourself," the boy returned.

"Well, somebody's to blame, and I'm in command," he said with finality. "I'm afraid our training is against us with Bedouins."

"Why is that?"

"Well, they never give notice of when they intend to fight. They just sneak up, like the wild desert animals they are."

"But my father often told me the soldiers' code: 'Do not attack in the night like a cheat. Give battle only when you can be seen. Give warning of the combat in advance.' "

"Yes, that's the way we're taught. And yet I've often wondered if there's not something to be said for this irregular warfare of theirs."

"But it's a coward's way to fight."

Tety laughed. "Well, we say that because there are a great many of us and we have the benefit of discipline and training. But suppose we were the Bedouins, lacking the organization or the numbers to challenge an invading army. Would it not then be right for us to fight in any way we could in order to win?"

Aahmes scratched his head. He had never heard such thoughts expressed before. He had never encountered an Egyptian officer who put himself in the place of the enemy, to try to see the situation from his viewpoint. "I — I just can't imagine myself not being Egyptian," the boy stammered.

"No, and that's another of our problems. We're so certain we're the only worthwhile people in the world." He frowned and fell silent. After a few moments he sighed and concluded, "Anyway, our discussion's likely to prove fruitless. The Bedouins' next attack will be in sufficient force that no one in the camp will remain alive to set the Sudanese on their trail. By the way, you didn't see my slave when you entered, did you?"

"No, Tety. Was he in here with you?"

"Yes, he always sleeps at my feet. The poor wretch probably panicked, ran out and got himself cut down. I'll miss Sa-Mentu. He's been with me for years." They began to hear voices outside, whispering back and forth as if preparing for a final attack. "Well, lad, there appears to be very little hope for us. I wish I could offer you better prospects, but you're the son of a fine man, and I know you'd want me to tell you the truth. Let's prepare to die like true Egyptians."

"Then there's no chance of rescue?"

"I'm afraid not. No caravan's likely to stumble by to save us. They don't travel by night. Ours don't anyway. As an extra precaution I did send a patrol on ahead just after we bedded down for the night, but they're not due to return until sunrise and we'll both be dead long before then. At least they'll arrive in time to see that we get a proper Egyptian burial; that is, if the Bedouins don't drag us off and eat us."

"Will they do that?"

The soldier laughed. "No, I don't think so. We tend to attribute all sorts of barbarous acts to them simply because they're our enemies."

"Will they attack in the same way this time?"

"I doubt it. It's quiet out there now, so I suppose they're deciding on their next plan of battle. No, this time their tactics will be different. They haven't had much success sending in one or two at a time. And they can't flatten the tent because the poles are inside. So I imagine they'll attack from all sides, ripping holes everywhere and pouring in all at once."

Tety tousled the boy's hair. "At least," he finished with a sad smile, "it should be over quickly."

Aahmes was about to say that he wasn't afraid, even though it would have been a lie, when a noise from outside drew their attention. Wearily, he rose to take his place beside Tety. So this was it. This was how a soldier died, he thought. Had Horem-heb felt like this just before the Pharaoh's guard killed him? What would become of Khepri now? It looked as though Hemon had won and would manage the estate for his own advantage, as he had planned. The Great One would never learn the truth about Horem-heb. Tears sprang to Aahmes' eyes, but he dashed them away with the back of his free hand.

An arm reached in and pulled the flaps aside, and from all around the tent came the sound of stealthy feet approaching.

# RESCUE

A solitary figure slipped into the tent. It moved cautiously towards Tety and Aahmes. The commander raised his sword over his head. "Strike as though inspired by the evil Seth," he shouted.

"Captain," a voice cried out, "are you here?" It was an Egyptian!

Tety swung his blade aside, narrowly missing the man. "Tehuti?" he asked in surprise. "Is that really you?"

The other laughed. "Come and see for yourself," he replied, stepping back and raising the flap to let the moonlight stream in. Aahmes recognized one of the young patrol leaders he had seen the day before.

Tety seized the man and embraced him with a near-suffocating hug. "Tehuti," he repeated. "But I didn't expect to see you again until daylight."

The patrol leader smiled. "Indeed, captain. But from the appearance of the camp, I'd say we were needed, wouldn't you?"

The three of them stepped out into the moonlight, and Aahmes saw that the stealthy sounds they had heard had come from the rest of the army patrol. They had been stationed around the perimeter of the tent to prevent the escape of any Bedouins who might still be inside. "How did you know we needed you?" Tety asked the new arrival.

"Your servant Sa-mentu caught up to us and reported the attack on the caravan. We came as quickly as we could."

"And the others in the camp?" Tety inquired, looking around.

"Too late, I'm afraid, sir. You and the boy are the only ones left. The Bedouins must have had scouts out, because as soon as we approached, they drove off the herds and disappeared into the desert."

"Yes, that's like them all right. They kill like poisonous vipers, then vanish like the birds of the Nile during the Season of Sowing."

At that moment they were interrupted by the approach of Tety's servant, Sa-mentu. The old man hobbled slowly towards his master. His happiness at arriving in time was so great that tears welled in his eyes.

"Old friend!" Tety greeted him, flinging his arms about him. "We have you to thank for our lives."

"My instructions from your father," the old man

began, gasping to catch his breath, "were to look after his son. But he didn't tell me I'd have to fight my way through an army of thieves and murderers and be bumped and jostled halfway across the desert to do it!"

The soldier laughed and patted the old man on the back. "What happened, foster-father? Tell me, for I may have to enroll you as a soldier too. As you can see, I haven't many left."

"When those savages crept into the camp, I was down at the other end, near the chariots," he began. "Sekhmet, your driver, had just returned from patrolling the camp, as you'd instructed, and the horses were still hitched to his chariot. He asked me where the guard had gone. I hadn't any idea, although he'd been standing near us just moments before. When one of the Bedouins leaped out at us from behind a sand dune, Sekhmet seized me by the arm and pulled me up onto the chariot, at the same time lashing the horses. I didn't want to leave you, master," Sa-mentu explained, "but I wouldn't have been any use to you with a blade in my hand, and besides, I knew the direction your patrol had gone."

"You did right, old friend."

Tears sprang to the man's eyes. "I was so worried about you, Tety, master, I scarcely noticed the ride. Sekhmet handed the reins to me so that he could fight off the Bedouins who tried to run at us and prevent our escape. The next thing I knew, he'd been hit and had fallen off, and I was left alone on that Seth-invented device. I was afraid I'd shake loose every bone in my body, but I was more concerned that I'd not get back in time with help."

"You timed your arrival perfectly, Sa-mentu. A few minutes more and we'd have been slaughtered too. So poor Sekhmet is dead. He was a brave man, and we fought the campaigns of the Great One together for many years." Tety stretched wearily and began touring the camp. Aahmes followed, fearful of viewing the grisly sight by himself. Somehow he seemed to absorb strength from the magnificent giant who had befriended him.

All the guards had been killed, they learned, along with every one of the merchants. Now and then they came upon the body of a Bedouin, but most of the attackers were inside the tent. Many of the soldiers had not even had a chance to draw their weapons. The boy shut his eyes against the horror.

When they had finished, Tety gave orders that all the dead were to be gathered and buried in a mass grave, and that markers were to be set up so that an army patrol could return and do the job properly later on. Because only a handful of men and a few donkeys remained to him, he didn't want to stay in the vicinity any longer than necessary. "The Bedouins are probably long gone," he told Aahmes. "Still I think we'd better move on just as rapidly as possible."

The sun was nearing its midday peak by the time they

finally got under way. Aahmes was given a donkey to ride. He tried to sleep on its back, but the animal's constant swaying prevented even rest, since most of the boy's energy was required just to stay on its back. And then there was the sun. It beat down unmercifully. The heat and glare made Aahmes dizzy, and once or twice he almost lost consciousness again. But he hung on. riding behind Tety and the old servant. It was a miserable day — one he was sure he would never forget.

By nightfall they had reached the next oasis. They found it already occupied by a large Egyptian caravan on its way home. Tety talked with its merchant leader, then called Aahmes to his tent. "My friend," he said, "the caravan leader has been to the frontier and is now bound for Memphis. According to him, and he has no reason to lie since money is not involved, the Pharaoh was called back to Egypt and is no longer on the frontier."

The boy's face fell. What was he to do now? "But Tety, I must find him," he pleaded.

"According to the merchant, the Pharaoh is headed for the royal capital of Lower Egypt — "

"That's Memphis," Aahmes said, hope rising.

"So it is, lad. I also hear that your brother has been taken there for trial. I've arranged with the merchant to take you there, if you wish to go. How you'll manage to see the Great One once you're there, I have no idea. I can't help you in that regard, but my prayers and wishes accompany you."

"Thank you, Tety. I don't know what to say."

"It's the least I can do for someone who saved my life," answered the captain. "The truth is, I'm getting a little tired of this nomadic goat-herding life. I wish I could go with you. Perhaps I'd be of some help — I think we make a pretty good pair."

"I wish you could too, Tety. But I understand that you have another duty. After all, I am the son of a soldier."

"Well, at least we may have taught a lesson to some of those Bedouins. Here is a silver ring, Aahmes. If you should be in need of money, you'll have no difficulty selling it. You might need some when you arrive in Memphis. It's a large city, with many government officials." He looked a little embarrassed. "Bribes," he added quietly.

"I understand, Tety, and I don't know what to say — or if I'll ever be able to repay you."

"Don't worry about that. The ring is nothing — I brought it back from my last campaign in Asia. As for helping you, I knew and respected your father. It's the very least I can do. Besides, my reward is in knowing that Egypt still produces brave young lads like you who do what they think best for their families, no matter what the cost to themselves. Come, the caravan will be waiting."

They rose, and Tety led Aahmes to the tent of the merchant, a fat, oily person whom Aahmes disliked immediately. But he had little choice in the matter. It might be weeks or even months before he met another caravan travelling straight to Memphis. And crossing the desert alone, he now knew, was out of the question.

Tety explained the boy's wishes to the merchant, who nodded his head in agreement. Then the captain shook the boy's hand and turned to leave. At the tent opening he stopped and looked back. "Remember, Khonsu," he said, "the boy is to be delivered *safely* to Memphis. If you do not keep your word, we're certain to meet again, and you know what I'll do to that throat of yours."

The merchant waddled forward. "Fear for nothing, oh mighty warrior of the king, oh great and courageous captain of the desert troops. I will honour our bargain. Am I not to be trusted?"

"Only when someone puts a dagger point to your belly," Tety answered. "Remember, I have a long arm and many friends in army garrisons across the country."

"Of course, great captain. You may depend upon me."

"If I can't, no one else will, ever again." The soldier raised his hand in a farewell salute and allowed the flap to fall back into place.

"Well, and this is the little one who wishes to cross the desert with us," the merchant began.

Tety had warned Aahmes that Khonsu would try to get information from him. "Just get me there, merchant," he replied. "That's all you need to know."

Khonsu bowed.

The caravan left at dawn the following morning. Tety had decided to stay over for an extra day so that his men could recover from their night march and the difficult journey of the previous day. He was waiting beside the road and waved to Aahmes as he passed on the back of a donkey. Neither said a word, for they shared the warrior's feelings of comradeship, which require no spoken expression.

Aahmes had been greatly refreshed by the night's rest and the prospect of being taken directly to the Pharaoh. Soon he would be in Memphis, and then he would have to find some way to reach the Great One. But the time to worry about crossing the Nile is after you have crossed all the canals that lead to it, he reminded himself. He would worry about getting into the Royal Palace once he had reached Memphis.

The caravan was on the road for three days, and not once did they see any trace of the Bedouins. Aahmes knew the desert nomads were never far away, were probably following their every move, but the caravan was guarded by a sizable force of Egyptian soldiers. It was too large for them to attack successfully.

As dawn broke over the desert on the fourth day, Aahmes was already saddling his donkey. He knew they were nearing the end of their journey. The members of the caravan were excited, for some of them had families in Memphis whom they had not seen for months. He rode near the head of the caravan now, just behind Khonsu, who also rode a donkey. The fat merchant changed mounts every hour or so, so that no beast would become overtired. Unfortunately he showed less thoughtfulness towards his workers, who staggered under the heavy loads he assigned them.

He caught sight of Aahmes and smiled. Again he tried to extract the reason for the boy's trip, but Aahmes said nothing except that he was anxious to reach the sacred city.

Reluctantly, the merchant gave up prying. Picking up stray bits of information was good business for him. Sometimes he was able to use them himself, and sometimes he sold them to interested individuals. At last, though, when he saw that the boy would volunteer nothing, he gave up.

Aahmes asked, "How far are we from Memphis?"

"Not far. In fact, when we reach the top of the next dune, you should be able to catch sight of the royal city."

Aahmes dug his heels into the donkey's side and they climbed the hill. Below lay the magnificent capital of Lower Egypt, the sacred city of Memphis.

# A CONSPIRACY

Aahmes thanked the merchant and bade farewell to the caravan as soon as he could upon reaching Memphis. He needed no directions to reach the Royal Palace, for it was tall and imposing. It stood in the centre of the city, surrounded by many temples. Six separate buildings represented the main divisions of government.

He felt that he would have little trouble getting in as far as the Vizier at least. Perhaps he could explain the problem to him since, as chief minister, he saw the Pharaoh every day and was in charge of arranging audiences with him.

Aahmes was nervous, but he did expect to be allowed to tell his story. What had he been taught at the Temple of Life about the role of the chief minister? *To be Vizier requires not mildness but firmness . . . Do not send away any petitioner unheard . . .* Yes, something like that. And he was certainly a petitioner.

He continued along the neat right-angled streets, past

the homes of the workers and beyond, into the walled area containing the buildings of the royal administration. They were laid out exactly as in Thebes, a city he had visited many times with his father. The treasury was situated on one side of the wide thoroughfare, and the law courts on the other. Farther down stood the chancellery office and the buildings devoted to agriculture, tax-collecting and war. Next to religion, these were the three most important concerns of Egyptian life.

Beyond these structures lay the temples, including one set aside for the private use of the Great One himself, where he prayed every day for the safety of Egypt. It was called the House of the Morning, Aahmes knew, and right next to it stood the Royal Palace. Looking about him at the many magnificent buildings, Aahmes was reminded once again of how the Gods had favoured Egypt over other nations.

Everywhere he went, he saw people from many walks of life — labourers, carpenters in their leather aprons, bare-footed peasants, stately priests with their heads shaved, and soldiers. Hundreds and hundreds of soldiers paraded through the streets, as though the Pharaoh were readying yet another campaign against the miserable Libyans. Despite his father's efforts, and that of many other Egyptians for as far back as he knew, there were always frontiers to defend and enemies to war against. All was as the Gods intended, he supposed.

His mind flew back to Tety, out there in the desert somewhere, warring for Egypt. Perhaps someday Aahmes would serve under such a commander. It would be an honour. But first, he reminded himself, the affairs of his family had to be straightened out, or he would end up as less than a peasant. He marched right on past the royal guards and into the palace, until he reached the Vizier's reception area.

It was well past midday, but a long row of people still waited patiently, because they knew each case would be dealt with in order. Aahmes remembered another precept he had copied out as a student. It said something about the Vizier granting audience to the person at the front of the line before he spoke to the one at the back. And also: *If you refuse a petitioner, let him know why. A man with a problem wants his tale to be heard sympathetically even more than he wants it put right.* Well, he certainly wanted a hearing, but he wanted his problem put right too.

The large room was jammed with a bewildering array of people — some black-skinned ones from Nubia, some fairer-skinned ones from Asia, and even some yellow-skinned ones from Horus knew where. Aahmes was fascinated by their strange and exotic clothing.

Every now and then a curly-haired Syrian in Egyptian dress entered the room to summon the next in line. From his hair, it was obvious he was not an Egyptian.

Besides, he wore a beard, and Egyptians were clean-shaven.

Since he could not find a seat, Aahmes rested on the floor between two other petitioners. There was no indication of how long he would have to wait, so he thought he might as well relax. No sense in being too tired to tell his story when his turn came. The heat of the day and the fatigue brought on by his adventures in the desert now began to catch up with him, however, and without intending to, he closed his eyes and drifted off into a much-needed sleep.

No one wakened the boy. Everyone just ignored him and moved along to take his turn until it was announced that the Vizier would listen to no more petitions that day. Those who had not yet been heard stood up resignedly and left the palace, paying no attention to the lone boy asleep between two benches against the wall.

When he awoke, it was already growing dark and the reception hall was deserted. Before he could get up to see where everyone had gone, the man with the curly hair and beard entered the room carrying a torch. The light made weird shadows dance eerily along the high walls and on the ceiling. Aahmes was about to say something when he saw that the Syrian was not alone. Behind him stood a similar-looking man, only with a shorter beard. They were speaking to each other in low voices.

"When is it to be, Maharbaal?"

"Tonight." The other paused and looked about cautiously to make certain the room was deserted. Neither saw Aahmes, who remained perfectly still. They were speaking in Syrian, the language that Anath-herte had taught him.

"And the guards?"

"The guards were doubled for only a short time after that fool Horem-heb stumbled onto our plan."

"Yes, that was awkward. But now we're ready?"

"Yes. Several of the guards are on our side this time. And so is the Steward of the Harem, the Captain of the Bowmen, and the Fan-bearer to His Majesty."

"Is everything arranged?"

"Tonight Ramses is to sleep alone. We'll enter the royal chamber while he sleeps, and he will die."

Aahmes was paralysed with fear. Now there was no chance of seeing the Vizier. If this man served him, the chief minister himself might be part of the plan. But what he had heard had served to explain his father's actions. Horem-heb had been trying to save the Pharaoh, not harm him. Somehow he had discovered the evil scheme, most likely just as it was about to be put into effect, and had rushed to the Pharaoh's side fully armed, in order to protect him. Probably the guards had lost their nerve at the sight of his father and had killed him, pretending that he was the one who was trying to harm the Great One.

But what was Aahmes to do with this knowledge? How could he get word to the Pharaoh to warn him? And even if he arrived in time, would the Great One believe him? Or would he be cut down just as his father had been? Then everyone would be convinced of Khepri's guilt and he would certainly be killed and thrown to the crocodiles.

He huddled down between the benches as best he could, staying as quiet as possible. Would the two Syrians remain here, he wondered, or would they leave soon? Once they had gone, he could sneak out and search for some way to warn the Pharaoh.

The men continued to talk. From the conversation, Aahmes gathered that Maharbaal was the Vizier's secretary and that he was one of the leading conspirators. The name of the other man was not mentioned.

After a few minutes they separated. Maharbaal walked back into the main palace, and his friend strolled past the young eavesdropper's hiding-place and left through the front door. As soon as the boy was sure he was alone, he rose and hurried out of the building in the same direction.

Night had fallen by now, and except for an occasional guard and one or two priests returning to the temple, the courtyard was deserted. Aahmes had to find some place to sit and think.

He walked down a side street and seated himself on the stone steps of one of the smaller temples. What was he to do now? Was there any way he could reach the Pharaoh? Someone had to warn him, and that was a task no one else but he could undertake because very likely nobody else knew, except those who were part of the plot. If only Tety were here. Or Khepri. They would know what to do. They would save the Pharaoh somehow. Somewhere in this very city at this very hour Khepri was being held prisoner, and Aahmes had no way of knowing where. If only he could talk to him, that might help. But there was no use worrying about what could not be.

As he settled himself more comfortably on the steps, there was a slight movement behind him. What was it? He froze, not knowing whether he should turn to look or simply run away.

There it was again — a scraping sound like that of soft leather against a stone step. The hairs stood up on the back of Aahmes' neck. He leaned forward as if he were about to run; but instead, he rolled rapidly to one side. As he did so, a figure lunged toward the spot where he had been sitting, landing heavily at the bottom of the steps.

In moments the man had recovered and was on his feet facing the boy. Aahmes recognized the Syrian who had been talking to Maharbaal in the palace. The man must have seen him crouched between the benches. But

why had he given no evidence of it at the time? Oh well, there was no time to think about that now.

His attacker had drawn a knife and was slowly advancing up the steps. The boy was frightened, but he did not dare call for help. Even if the police came, he would no doubt be arrested along with the Syrian. Precious time would be lost while he explained, and even then there was no way of knowing whether his story would be believed. Probably the Syrian would be released as soon as he identified himself as a friend of the secretary of the Vizier. And Aahmes would be held prisoner while the Great One was murdered in his sleep.

No, he had to deal with this himself. As the man advanced up the steps, Aahmes retreated towards the top. He attempted to stay beyond the range of the other's blade, but slowly the Syrian worked his way up to the same level and struck at him. Stepping backwards, the boy lost his footing and fell heavily. As he lay with his head on one step and his feet above him on the next, the man turned on him, smiling in a sinister way at finding himself so near success. Then he took another step. As he did so, Aahmes thrust one foot forward and lashed out with the other. The man lost his balance and tumbled headlong down the steps, screaming. He landed with a bump and lay in a crumpled heap on the road.

The boy wasted no time. His assailant's screams would soon bring someone out. He had to be gone before anyone arrived. Scrambling down the steps, he retrieved the knife and hurried off into the darkness.

Behind him he heard the sound of voices, but he paid no attention. He was armed now, and in possession of very dangerous information. He had no choice but to force his way in to see the Great One. It was the only way he would ever be able to solve his family's problems, to say nothing of saving the Pharaoh's life.

# INSIDE THE PALACE

There was so little time!

Aahmes raced back to the building where he had spent the afternoon. Thanks to the sleep he had had there, he at least felt rested. He was going to need all his strength for the task that lay ahead.

Approaching the palace at a dead run, he slipped into the shadow cast by one of the nearby temples. A side stairway led up the pyramid-shaped structure, and keeping under cover, he silently climbed towards the entrance. He was a third of the way up when he spotted a guard at the door. Without being seen, he retreated to the bottom step again to decide on his next move.

What was he to do? Somehow he had to gain entry to the Royal Palace,, for there, somewhere in its inner depths, the Pharaoh was preparing for bed, or might already have retired. Unless Aahmes reached him, he would never see another dawn.

Noticing some scattered stones under his feet,

Aahmes bent down and scooped them together until he had a handful. Cautiously he climbed to where he had first spotted the guard, keeping well to the shadows which were shortening with the rising moon. He crept up as far as he could without leaving his shelter; then with a sudden movement, he flung the stones in the direction of the soldier. They landed on the steps, and the man turned sharply at the sound. Aahmes wished he had another handful, but it was too late to think of that now. The soldier hesitated for some moments. Finally, his mind made up, he left his post to investigate.

Should there not be at least two guards? Perhaps the other had gone to investigate the Syrian's scream. Hesitantly the soldier came down the steps, gripping his spear tightly. He reached the area where the stones had landed and stood there looking puzzled.

At that moment Aahmes leaped from the shadows and made a dash for the door. Before the guard could stop him, he had darted through it and was racing along the wide corridor. At the end of it he paused briefly to orient himself. Yes, the palace looked very much like the one in Thebes. Although he had not been inside that one himself, his father had often described its layout to him.

Aahmes could not afford to stop for long. He plunged through a door that led to another long hallway, turned left and headed towards what should be the sleeping quarters — if he remembered correctly what his father had told him. He wished he had listened more carefully.

He passed the large reception room where the Pharaoh received those visitors and ambassadors who managed to persuade the Vizier to arrange an audience for them, and moved into a narrower corridor. These should be the servants' quarters. Cautiously he opened a door. Yes, there were several sleeping forms on the beds inside the room. From their clothing, he recognized them as servants. He shut the door and proceeded down the hall again.

He should soon be reaching the entrance to the harem, where the Pharaoh's many wives stayed. Sure enough, there it was at the end of the next corridor. Two guards stood at the door. Aahmes paused where he was, concealed by the curtains that lined the walls. Somehow he had to make his way past those guards, for he knew that the royal bed chamber lay just beyond the harem. He would have to be quick too. It would not be long before the soldier at the entrance raised the alarm. Strange it hadn't happened already.

Aahmes considered his problem, wondering how Tety or Khepri or even Horem-heb would have solved it. Even if he created a disturbance, only one of the soldiers would come to investigate. And if he got past that one, there would still be the other to deal with. Yet he felt a new confidence in his ability to handle difficult situations. He had faced many over the past few days and had managed to overcome them all. He had no intention of turning back now.

To go on would mean risking death. But he had done that several times already — swimming the Nile, crossing the desert, warning Tety, fighting the Bedouins, and even tonight, confronting his assailant on the steps of the temple.

As these thoughts ran through his head, one hand dropped to the hilt of the knife he had picked up from the Syrian. What would happen to him now, so near the royal bed chamber with a weapon in his possession? The guards would assume, or pretend to assume, that he had come to complete what his father had attempted. He would be cut down on the spot. Worse still, these evil men might kill him, then take his blade and use it on the Pharaoh, blaming the whole thing on Aahmes' family. And they would have his corpse as proof.

Aahmes debated with himself about getting rid of the knife. Finally he decided that if he were captured he would be killed either way, armed or unarmed. So he might as well at least have something to defend himself with.

Large vases stood at regular intervals along the corridor, some of them nearly as tall as Aahmes himself. He crept along the folds of the curtains until he was directly behind one of them. Then he put his shoulder to it, and with his feet braced against the wall, managed to topple it. Before the heavy vase had crashed to the floor, he was hiding behind the next one, nearer the harem entrance. One of the guards hurried along the hall to see what had knocked the vase over. When he was safely on the other side of Aahmes' hiding place, the boy crept rapidly along the curtained corridor until he was almost at the door. Then he jumped out and raced towards it.

He swung his foot sharply at the shin of the soldier who had remained at his post. Caught by surprise, the men yelped in pain and grabbed for his leg, dropping his spear. As he hopped about on one foot, Aahmes shoved him so hard that he fell to the floor. Without pausing to look back, the boy ran into the harem.

From everywhere came the sounds of women talking and laughing. As Aahmes passed one of the doors, it was swung open by a pretty young girl. He paid no attention to her. A slave emerged from another room and tried to block his path, but Aahmes dodged and slipped past him. Several women emerged from various rooms to see what was happening, but the boy did not stop running. As he neared the end of the hall, two more soldiers appeared before him. Just as he noticed them, another door opened beside him. He threw himself into the room, nearly knocking a young girl off her feet. Before she could recover, Aahmes clamped a hand over her mouth. "Say nothing, and you won't be hurt!" he told her.

Her beautiful eyes looked startled, but she did not seem really afraid. Outside, he heard the guards hurrying past. "Is the Great One's room that way?" he asked gesturing with his head.

She nodded.

"Good. If I release you, I want you to promise by Horus you won't call out."

She nodded her agreement and he took his hand away from her mouth. But as soon as he did, she leaped towards the door, flung it open and let out an ear-piercing scream.

The guards turned. But they were not quick enough to catch Aahmes as he brushed past the girl and dashed through the large door leading into the royal bed chamber. He swung it closed behind him and fitted the latch into place. He hoped that would hold the guards for at least a few minutes.

He found himself in a huge room containing a single large bed against one wall. On the bed lay a sleeping figure. The room was lighted by several alabaster oil lamps, which flickered and cast weird shadows against the high walls.

The royal guards were already at the door, pounding on it. Aahmes rushed over to the bed, and as he did so, the sleeping man turned suddenly, startling the boy. "Who is there?" he called out. "Who dares to break in unsent for upon the rest of the Pharaoh?"

A large fat man struggled to a sitting position.

Aahmes stopped at the foot of the bed and said, "Your Majesty, it is I, Aahmes."

The Pharaoh relaxed slightly when he saw it was only

a boy. "Aahmes, you say? Do I know you, Aahmes? Do you realize you are in the Royal Palace and that this is the King's bed chamber?"

"I know where I am, Your Majesty. But you do not know me. I am the son of Horem-heb."

"Horem-heb? Horem-heb, you say? Why, he was my general who — "

The Pharaoh reached under his headrest and drew out a sword. "Have you come to finish what your father began?"

"Yes, Your Majesty, but not to harm you. I've come to warn you that others plan to kill you this very night."

"Kill me? And how do you know this, Aahmes?" As the boy sought for words to explain, the Pharaoh added impatiently, "Be not silent, be not silent. Thy name is pronounced."

"Your Majesty, I . . . " And then the whole story came out. The death of his father, the burial by Khepri, the treatment he had received at school, the disloyalty of Hemon, his swimming of the Nile and his flight into the desert, the meeting with Tety, the Bedouin attack, the caravan journey back to Memphis, his hearing of the assassination plot, his fight with the Syrian, and finally his adventures in the palace. When he had finally finished, the Great One rose from his bed and strode across the room. The pounding on the door continued, but no one had called out any warning to the Pharaoh.

"And you have been through all this to warn me? I

believe your story, Aahmes. To tell the truth, I did not think Horem-heb meant to harm me. He had served me faithfully all his life. But he was already dead, you see, and I left it at that. I did not think of the effect it would have on his family. Here, boy, help me to arm myself."

Aahmes hurried to his side. The Pharaoh took up his sword as if he still knew how to use it, despite his age and weight. "Will you fight beside your King, boy?" Aahmes drew his dagger and took his place. "Good." Ramses snorted. "We'll show them that we're not wild beasts to be cut down without so much as a fight."

Something heavy was being hurled against the door now, and it was beginning to crack. Soon one panel was out and another was split. Aahmes remembered that the guards were in on the plot. He watched, fascinated, as the door finally splintered. Through the opening he caught a glimpse of the evil bearded face of Maharbaal.

# TRAPPED!

Besides Maharbaal, Aahmes could see a tall woman, two or three soldiers and an officer outside the door. When the opening was large enough, one of the soldiers squeezed through. He rushed at the Pharaoh with his sword drawn, but Ramses turned the blade aside and began fencing with him. Soon another soldier was through the hole as well, and hurrying to join the fight.

Aahmes leaped into his path, knife ready. The guard paused for an instant, and then took a slash at his head. The boy ducked and retreated a single step. His opponent advanced to the attack, trying to force him back against the wall. Aahmes kept moving, weaving back and forth and occasionally lunging forward with the knife. Each time he pulled up before he reached his target. The soldier gained confidence from this, thinking that his young adversary was afraid to follow through. He closed in and once again swiped at the boy's head. While his defence was down, Aahmes caught him squarely with his knife. A puzzled look spread over the man's features as he slowly sank to his knees.

Looking up, Aahmes saw that the Pharaoh was being closely pressed by the officer. The boy turned the blade around in his hand and threw it at the man, narrowly missing him. Retrieving the sword that had fallen at his feet, he ran to help.

The Pharaoh was perspiring freely and breathing heavily, but he seemed to remember how to use a weapon. He was parrying the officer's sword with some skill. However, before Aahmes could reach his side, the officer had shortened his weapon and stabbed it into the Great One. Ramses fell back hard against the wall, but managed to keep his feet. Just as the man raised his sword to strike again, the boy caught him from behind. He staggered into Ramses, who pushed him aside, then yelled, "Look out!"

Before Aahmes could heed the warning, he found himself in the grip of Maharbaal's powerful arms. He was now unarmed, but he kicked back as hard as he could with his foot, forcing the Syrian to release him. The woman, who had been watching from the doorway, threw Maharbaal a spear. He lunged forward with it, but the boy managed to dodge the sharp point. The Syrian lunged again and this time caught Aahmes on the arm, slicing it to the bone. Aahmes reached up to cover the wound, trying vainly to staunch the flow of blood. Again the point was directed at him, but he leaped to one side and wrestled for a grip on the spear. Unfortunately Maharbaal was bigger, more powerful and unhurt. He easily twisted it out of his young opponent's grasp.

As Aahmes retreated, the other advanced on him, waiting his chance. He struck out again, and in trying to avoid the blow, the boy tripped over one of the soldiers on the floor. He fell heavily, and Maharbaal swung the spear at him with all his might. Aahmes pulled back, but not before he had received a wound in the leg. He winced with pain and tried rolling away, but he realized that his position was hopeless.

He was caught now. The Syrian reached down to pick up a fallen sword. Slowly and deliberately he advanced.

This is probably the very man who killed my father, Aahmes thought, and now he's going to kill me too. But what could he do? He was weak from fatigue and loss of blood. There wasn't even any way to save the Pharaoh now. As soon as Maharbaal had finished with him, he would kill the Great One too. Well, he had tried. And at least they would travel to the Celestial Fields together. Still, he could have cried with rage at himself for failing. The thought of dying did not bother him as much as the thought that he had come so far and had so nearly succeeded . . .

The Syrian stood over him, his sword raised to strike the final blow.

"Hold!" called a voice from the doorway.

All eyes turned to see who dared to interfere. But Aahmes recognized the voice. "Tety!" he cried.

At first he was not certain it was really his friend standing in the open doorway. Perhaps he had prayed so hard for help to come that now he was imagining it. But it *was* Tety, with a troop of soldiers at his back. He strode into the room, signalling his men to remain in the hallway.

Thinking quickly, Maharbaal lowered his sword arm and said to Tety, "Look, Captain, I have just captured this boy who struck the Pharaoh." Aahmes glanced over and saw that the Great One had slid to the floor and lay there unconscious — or even dead. If the Pharaoh did not live to explain what had happened, it would be Aahmes' word against that of the Vizier's secretary. Tety continued to advance and the Syrian went on quickly, "I was going to save the law courts some trouble."

"With what? The spear or the sword? I happen to know this boy, and if there's been a plot against the Great One I find it considerably easier to believe *you're* behind it, my friend."

Maharbaal looked towards the doorway for a sympathetic face, but found none. "Wait. Surely you don't believe the word of a boy against that of the Vizier's secretary?"

"In this case I do."

Maharbaal was cornered and he knew it. He spread

his hands in a placating gesture. "Surely you don't mean — " he began. But even as he spoke, he spun around and thrust the sword in Aahmes' direction. Before the blow could land, Tety struck him, diverting his arm and sending him sprawling onto the Pharaoh's bed. The captain picked up the sword that Maharbaal had dropped and tossed it to him. "Here," he challenged him. "Let's see how good you are against a healthy man."

The Syrian drew himself slowly to his feet. Then, swinging the blade wildly, he rushed towards Tety, who ducked two or three blows then pushed him away with his free hand.

"Come on. Surely you can do better than that. You're very skilful at murdering innocent children and sleeping men. At least try to put up a fight."

The secretary stopped to catch his breath, a look of sheer hatred on his face. Suddenly he yelled and rushed forward again, only to have his blow parried and to find himself once more pushed backward. He almost lost his balance, but Tety's strong arm reached out and steadied him.

Slashing blindly at the soldier's hand, Maharbaal attacked again. This time, instead of stepping aside or parrying the blow, Tety closed in and struck the Syrian. Pain crowded the hatred from the conspirator's face as he staggered back a couple of steps, tumbled onto the bed and then rolled to the floor.

Immediately Sa-Mentu burst through the door and ran to the Pharaoh, examining him briefly. "He's badly hurt," he called over his shoulder. "Lift him onto the bed." Several of Tety's soldiers sprang to obey the orders.

When the Pharaoh's regular doctor had been sent for, Sa-Mentu hurried over to the wounded boy, who was being supported in a sitting position by the captain.

"Oh, Tety," Aahmes said, "I owe you so much. But what if the Great One should die? Who'll believe my story then?"

"Don't worry, lad. I'll do all in my power to clear your name."

"And I'll do what I can to heal those wounds of yours," added the servant.

"The Pharaoh still lives," someone called from the corner.

A slow smile spread over Aahmes' face as he lay back against the cool floor. Perhaps everything would turn out all right. Tety stood over him giving orders to the soldiers, while Sa-Mentu treated his arm and leg. That was all he remembered, for the next moment he slid into unconsciousness.

# THE COLLAR OF VALOUR

For several days Aahmes lay on a cot in the army barracks near the Royal Palace. There were times when he stirred and seemed on the point of waking, but each time he settled down and slept again. Sa-Mentu stayed by him constantly and even slept in the same room. Under such excellent care it could only be a matter of time before the boy recovered.

When he finally regained consciousness, the first sight to greet his eyes was the faithful servant mixing a medicine consisting of cinnamon and castor oil. When he saw the patient awaken, Sa-Mentu handed him the cup. Aahmes gulped the mixture down quickly, remembering the unpleasant taste of any medicine he had ever had before.

"That's the way," encouraged the servant. "You're looking much better than you did yesterday and the day before."

"Yesterday? The day before? How long have I been

here?"

"This is the fourth morning since the night you broke into the Royal Palace," Sa-mentu explained.

"Fourth morning! Have I slept for that long?"

"Yes, with a little help from my medicines."

The boy looked down and noticed that his wounded leg and arm had been expertly bandaged.

"You'll have no trouble with your wounds now. They'll heal as good as new," Sa-Mentu assured him.

Aahmes leaned back to rest, then sat bolt upright again. "But what about the Great One? Have you heard any news?"

"Not since last night. He's been very ill. His best doctors have been called in and they've worked over him steadily, but I'm afraid the wound is very deep. He's no longer a young man, you know."

Aahmes' heart sank. Had he come so far, through so many adventures, only to fail in the end? The Great One knew the full story and he would be the one with the authority and the desire to correct the wrongs done to Horem-heb and Khepri. But what if the Great One died? Would all his efforts have been in vain? So far as the boy knew, he himself might be under arrest.

"Sa-Mentu, where are we?" he inquired.

"This is an army barracks."

So he was right. He had been arrested. Probably Tety had arranged that he should be taken here rather than to a regular prison. He guessed the rest.

"Has the Pharaoh not regained consciousness then?" he asked.

"I don't believe so. At least he hadn't by last evening."

There it was. The only one who could have helped was incapable of doing so. Unless the Pharaoh woke up long enough to explain Aahmes' presence in his room, he was in very serious trouble. He knew that the laws of Egypt made no allowance for age. In a case of treason you were either guilty or not guilty. And the penalty was death. Now his family would never be reunited in the Celestial Fields. If only he had done a better job of protecting the Great One!

"Anyway — " the old servant began, then stopped as the door opened. Looking up, they saw Tety enter the room.

"Hello there, little one," he said. "You certainly are a determined fellow."

"Tety, have you heard any word?"

"Ah, now, let me see. Where will I start? Well, a great many arrests have been made. At least fifty or more. It was quite a widespread plot you stumbled on."

"I mean the Pharaoh. How is he?"

The soldier's face hardened. "Not well, I'm afraid. His physicians expect that very shortly he will assume the shape of Horus and fly to the heavens."

So it was true. His worst fears had proved right. The Great One was to die. "I — I liked him," he said simply, "although I scarcely knew him."

"Yes, I think I know what you mean. He was a fair-minded man. When he awoke last night — "

"He awoke?"

Tety stopped. "Why, yes. Didn't you know? But of course not. How could you? Yes, he regained consciousness and was very anxious to talk."

"Did he mention — my family?"

"In great detail. I was there. He had many fine things to say about you, your brother and your father."

The boy relaxed and leaned back. Everything was going to work out after all, he thought, as relief flooded through him.

The commander smiled down at him. "You know, you must promise to serve in my regiment when you're older. I've never met a lad who was so intent on accomplishing his purpose regardless of the risks to himself. We'll have great fun together defending the frontiers of Egypt."

"Oh, Tety, there's nothing I would rather do!"

"We might even make a habit of crossing the desert together — just the two of us, and Sa-Mentu. Those poor Bedouins don't know what they're in for."

"Oh, no. You may leave me out, master," muttered the servant.

But, Sa-Mentu, what would we do without you, just in case there were more than we could handle? Who'd drive the chariot to summon help?"

"I've had enough, thank you. My bones are getting too old for that sort of thing."

"Listen to him. If I were to leave for the frontier this very moment, he'd follow me gladly — even if I went without my regiment."

"So would I!" exclaimed Aahmes.

"I know you would," said Tety. "But I think I'd better leave for now and let you rest some more."

"First tell me about the plotters. What will become of them?"

"Oh, yes, the plotters. Well, many of them were women from the Royal Harem."

"But why would they betray the king?"

"That's a very old story. One of the junior wives named Tiy thought her boy, Pentewere, should succeed Ramses. Since the throne had been promised to another of the Pharaoh's sons, the only way that could happen was for Ramses to be killed and his throne seized."

"Do you mean that one of the Pharaoh's own children was part of this plot?"

"That's it. His mother began enlisting supporters — the Chief of the Chamber, Pebekkamen, and a royal butler named Mesedsure, an overseer of the treasury, an army general named Peyes, various royal scribes, the wives of the officers of the harem gate, and a number of others, including the ones you discovered."

"But how were they all found out?"

"Oh, there are ways. The Pharaoh appointed a

special commission to investigate, and any living conspirators were tortured until the truth was extracted from them."

"Will they all be found guilty?"

"Strangely enough, the Pharaoh acted very cautiously in that matter. The commission was instructed to be very careful. He said, 'As for the words which the people have spoken, I know them not. Go you and examine them. When you have examined them, you shall cause to die by their own hand those who should die, without my knowing it. You shall execute punishment upon the others likewise, without my knowing it. Give heed and have a care lest you execute punishment upon anyone unjustly.' "

"That certainly sounds fair. How will they be executed?"

"Those who possess royal blood will be allowed to kill themselves. The son and wife, and probably the general, will be offered the chance to take poison. The rest will probably be put to death in the old way."

"You mean . . . "

"Yes. Bound hand and foot and thrown into the river for the crocodiles."

Aahmes swallowed. It was certainly a horrible punishment, and yet the crime had been a horrible one too. There was no way of knowing what tragedies might have been thrust upon Egypt if the king had died immediately. Would the new king chosen by a harem have been able to keep out the foreign invaders? Or would a new means of succession to the throne have been adopted, to be used in the future whenever some wife was displeased with the position accorded her son? Fortunately the Pharaoh had survived — at least long enough to give some directions.

Aahmes had one more important question for Tety. "What about my brother Khepri," he asked.

"Ah, yes. I knew there was something else I wanted to tell you. The Great One authorized his immediate release. His name is completely cleared, as is that of your father. Your estates are to be returned to you at once, and that guilty steward of yours is to be arrested. Oh, and you have been awarded the Golden Collar of Valour, just as your father was. The Pharaoh also sent a message that you are to be re-admitted to your school, and that an opening is to be kept for you to become an officer of the chariot corps as soon as you are old enough."

Aahmes was thrilled. He did not know what to say. He tried to get up, but Tety moved to his side and gently pushed him back. "No, my foolish young friend, you're not to move until the doctor here says you're ready to. Your brother will be waiting for you. As soon as he's had a chance to rest and clean up, he will probably come to see you."

Tety walked to the door. "Meanwhile, you get some more rest. You're going to need all your strength for the journey home." He turned to leave, then stopped again. "Oh, by the way, the Great One granted you one more honour."

"Oh? What?"

"A title — a new title you can be proud of. Instead of always introducing yourself as 'Aahmes, son of Horemheb,' now you can say, 'Aahmes, Sword of Egypt.' "

# RETURN TO LUXOR

It was nearly a month later before Aahmes was well enough to undertake the journey upriver to Luxor again. As each day passed he became increasingly restless and anxious to leave Memphis, but Sa-Mentu refused to allow him to travel until his wounds were properly healed. And so he waited impatiently, anxious to be off but also sorry at the prospect of leaving his new friends.

Tety and Khepri dropped in every day and spent many hours describing their various activities. Khepri had been reinstated in the army, but had been granted leave. Tety was also on leave, because he was soon to return to the frontier. This time he would lead a much larger group of soldiers, since he had been promoted to the rank of troop commander. Although Tety was always light-hearted and joking, Aahmes could tell that life in the royal capital did not appeal to him. He was anxious to get back to the business he knew so well — fighting. Khepri too was excited about rejoining his old regiment.

In a few years Aahmes would be enrolled in the chariot corps too. Meanwhile he was to return to school at the Temple of Life. The Pharaoh believed that an officer should know how to read and write just as well as the scribes, so that he would not be dependent on them to interpret and send messages. Reluctantly the boy agreed. But someday, someday soon, he would be off to join a regiment of his own. The greatest joy he could imagine would be for him and Khepri to command the wings of the army, with Tety in charge of the infantry in between.

Despite his own wound and his steadily worsening condition, the Great One had occasionally sent food to Aahmes from his personal kitchens. He had showered the boy with many other marks of his personal favour as well, including a visit from his own physician. At his direction, Horem-heb's body had been removed to the sacred precincts of the temple in Luxor. There it was being readied for the burial ceremony, which would take place after Aahmes and Khepri arrived home. The priests needed time to prepare the body, as well as all the proper prayers and inscriptions that were to be placed in the tomb.

The only problem that remained was Hemon. Although his arrest had been ordered, Khepri had prevented it for the time being. As he had explained to Aahmes, he was anxious to see the startled expression on the face of the steward when they told their story and confronted him with his guilt.

Finally Aahmes was pronounced strong enough to undertake the journey to Luxor. Sa-Mentu told him that his brother had already been sent for, and that all the preparations for the journey had been arranged by the Great One himself.

Aahmes leaped out of bed, but soon discovered that during his enforced rest his muscles had grown soft. For a few moments he found it difficult to retain his balance, but somehow he managed to stand straight. Any sign of weakness might cause him to be re-examined and forced to remain for a further period of time.

He thanked Sa-Mentu for all he had done; then with the servant by his side, he walked along the hallway that led to the main entrance of the barracks. This was the way his brother would probably come, and he did not want to miss him. Now that they were going home at last, he wanted no further delays.

The courtyard was bathed in early morning sunlight. Aahmes blinked, unaccustomed to the outdoors after his long weeks in bed. At the foot of the steps a chariot waited, the horses' reins held tightly by a groom. Beside it stood Khepri, who had by now regained most of the colour he had lost as a result of his imprisonment. He waved to Aahmes, and the boy limped down the last few steps to join him.

He stopped beside the chariot and turned around to survey the royal city. "Well, brother," he commented, "I won't really be sorry to leave here."

"No, I suppose not." Khepri helped him step up into the chariot. "Some of your adventures here have been far from pleasant. But you behaved well, little one."

Aahmes smiled. "I was only trying to help, Khepri."

"I wonder how many boys would have risked so much in the process. Somehow I don't think your friends at school would have taken all the chances you did. They'll certainly treat you differently when you return."

Yes, there was no doubt about that. Their attitude would be very different once they had heard the whole story. They would probably hang their heads in shame, especially Kames, who had been his best friend.

For the first time the two brothers noticed a group of priests who had emerged from a nearby temple. Four of them were carrying crates containing geese. They advanced to the middle of the square and placed the wooden containers on the ground, each facing a different direction. There appeared to be three or four of the long-necked birds in each. One of the priests walked slowly around them in a large circle, waving a stick of burning incense. Then, one by one, the crates were opened. As the first group of geese was released, the head priest intoned, "Hasten towards the south and tell the Gods of the South that the Pharaoh Ramses has taken the Double Crown." The birds flew off, heading south. The process was repeated, with birds heading north, east and west.

Aahmes watched in silence, fascinated by this religious rite that he had never before witnessed. "What does it mean?" he asked.

Until they were lost to sight, Khepri gazed in silence at the birds; then he turned to his brother. Placing a hand on his shoulder, he said quietly, "I'm afraid it means bad news, little one. Last night the Great One assumed the shape of Horus. He's gone to the Celestial Fields. This is the ceremony whereby the Two Lands are informed there is a new Pharaoh. His name is also Ramses and he has taken his father's place, as was intended all along."

Aahmes hung his head in sadness. He had known the Great One for only a short time, but he felt he would have liked him very much. And now he was gone. Seeing his concern, Khepri added, "You can be very proud of the fact that you helped to ensure the proper succession."

Yes, that was true. The appointed king sat on the throne of the Two Lands and Aahmes had helped to protect his right to it. He hoped that Ramses IV would make as good a ruler as his father had.

Climbing up behind him on the chariot, Khepri signalled the groom to release the reins, and the horses trotted away from the barracks. As slowly as possible, so that no sudden bump would jar his brother's wounds, he guided the chariot through the gates of the royal city, past the workers' houses and down to the harbour where a ship had been provided by the Pharaoh as one of his final acts of kindness towards them.

As they prepared to board, Khepri asked, "Are you glad to be going home?"

"Yes. I'm in quite a hurry to settle with Hemon."

"That will be the first thing, brother."

"I hope he hasn't been too unkind to Anath-herte."

The soldier looked startled. "Anath-herte? Why should he harm her?"

Aahmes explained how she had helped him, and that she had even given him the amulet he wore about his neck. He fingered it again, wondering how much it had protected and helped him.

"So she risked Hemon's wrath to warn you," Khepri mused.

"Yes, brother."

"By Horus, if he's harmed her he'll wish he hadn't!"

"Aren't you showing unusual concern for a slave?" Aahmes laughed.

His brother blushed. "Well, it's the least we can do," he explained lamely, "after what she did for us. You never would have been able to win our release if she hadn't helped."

"Yes, I know. I've been thinking that. Perhaps we should do something for her. Could we send her back to her own people?"

"Not much chance of that," Khepri snapped. Then he added, "Not many of them were left alive after our last campaign. There wouldn't be any life for her in that desolate country anyway. But we'll set her free, of course. Then perhaps we can make her believe that Egypt is her real home." At the look in his brother's eye when he spoke of the girl, Aahmes suspected there might be a marriage feast in his father's house in a few months' time. He knew how Anath-herte felt about Khepri. But he said nothing; there were some things a brother should learn for himself.

They were just about to board the ship when another chariot thundered up to the dock. It was Tety, who had come to say goodbye. At sight of the friend with whom he had shared such adventures, Aahmes could scarcely keep the tears from his eyes.

The newly-promoted troop commander unbuckled his sword and held it out to him. "Here," he said. "I don't know anyone who would make better use of this for his family, for his friends or for Egypt." He escorted them aboard ship, bade them farewell, then disappeared in his chariot as rapidly as he had come.

"There goes a fine soldier," Khepri commented

"Yes, and a good friend," added his brother.

They turned their attention to the vessel as it prepared to get under way. There was a captain, a lookout at the prow, a pair of men to steer and ten rowers. At a wave from the captain, the ropes were cast off and the ship began to drift away from the shore. In mid-stream the sail was raised and the men began rowing to the sound of a flute.

Behind them the city of Memphis — the old royal city with a new Pharaoh about to ascend the throne — rapidly grew smaller. No sooner had its temples faded from view than Aahmes ran forward to the prow. However long it might take, he wanted to be the first to see Luxor — and home.

Bert Williams grew up in Toronto and Montreal where he held a variety of jobs before deciding that teaching would be his career, writing his hobby. He has been teaching in the elementary schools of Scarborough since 1954 and writing in his spare time for almost as long.

Although he started out to write adult mystery novels, Bert turned to children's stories when he heard his young son complain that the books he was expected to read were "boring." Since then he has published two juvenile historical novels (*Food for the Raven,* set in Viking Scandinavia, and *Master of Ravenspur,* set in England during the War of the Roses) and a contemporary novel about a Sasquatch (*The Rocky Mountain Monster,* set in British Columbia), besides this newest story about a young boy in Ancient Egypt. He has also written over a hundred articles and short stories, mostly for professional and historical journals.